ALL I WANTED WAS SUSHI BUT I GOT ABDUCTED BY ALIENS INSTEAD

BUBBLE BABES

PETRA PALERNO

CONTENTS

For Chaos Crew—and anyone else who ever wanted a well-placed sucker.

☆BEFORE OUR ADVENTURE BEGINS☆

I can't wait to introduce you to the world that lies within the pages of this book. I wanted to let you know three things before our adventure begins. First, this is a book with very adult content. The triggers are listed below. Second, this book has lots of spice. In fact, it's mostly spice. Proceed with caution. Third, now would be the time to activate your suspension of disbelief. I know, you already picked up a book called All I Wanted Was Sushi But I Got Abducted By Aliens Instead, I should trust that you know what you're getting yourself into. I hope you enjoy the ride as much as our main characters will.

XOXO, Petra

PS: Let the record show that Opal is a plus-sized babe.

☆=------------Trigger Warnings-----------=☆

This story contains scenes that may depict, mention, or discuss aliens, abduction, death, hostages, human trafficking, kidnapping, needles, murder, grief, blood, gore, pregnancy, sexual content, exhibitionism, voyeurism, breath play and drugging.

CHAPTER 1

☆THE TRAFFIC JAM☆

☆OPAL

I SLAM my foot hard into the space where I assume the alien's balls will be, at the apex of his legs. His three eyes bore into me as I do but don't register anything that looks like pain on his bulbous head.

"That might not be the spot, but I'll fucking find it if you don't get that damn needle away from me!" I yell as I twist my wrist free from his purple hand.

No, it was less of a hand and more of a sticky claw. As I get myself free from the odd appendage, I bump into the woman sitting next to me. Her arms are crossed against her chest, the teal stretchy compression garments we wear covering the important bits just barely, but I doubt she's trying to be modest. She looks like she would rather be anywhere else than next to me, the only ornery bitch here. She flips her red hair over her shoulder and sighs audibly before turning to me. Her eyes assess the situation she has tried her best to ignore until this moment.

"Is this your first time here? What's your name?" The annoyance in her tone breaks through the saccharine affectation she tries to use. She sounds like a seasoned diner waitress impatient for me to place my order.

"My first time?" I laugh as I kick toward the alien again.

His body is covered in gray coveralls but everything left uncovered is composed of purple and blue scales that, unlike a snake's, secrete the same sticky substance as his hands. He is short, my head nearly level with his while I sit. I scowl into his three fly-like eyes that protrude from his head. His tiny mouth frowns as he throws up his claws. A string of syllables fall from the alien's lips, and then the same phrase is repeated again.

"Is your translator chip working?" the gorgeous redhead asks.

"Listen lady, how the fuck would I know if my translator chip was working or not?"

"Well, can you understand him?" She gestures to our purple captor. "And it's not lady, my name is Jessy."

"Jessy, darling," I respond with sarcasm dripping from my every word, "if my translator chip was working I wouldn't be trying my best to kick this fucker in the balls, now would I?"

Jessy turns to the alien with the ever elusive balls and lets the same sounding syllables out of her own lips. It sounds like no language I'd ever heard before. Jessy reaches toward me, and I instinctively flinch away.

"Jesus you're jumpy, just let me turn on your chip."

I relax, but only slightly, as her finger taps the space behind my ear three times. A painful static whizzes through my head, and I can't help but bring my hands to cover them. As I do, I feel the sharp prick of the syringe as it pierces my thigh.

"For being such a pain in my ass, you get extra." The bloops and clips of the alien's language are suddenly transformed into English. His accent isn't quite right, but I understand him all the same.

"Fuck you." I flip the nasty alien the bird as he moves down the aisle.

Rows of women are lined up on what feels like a bus, a space bus. A main aisle runs down rows of hard molded plastic seats wide enough for two girls each. If not for the fact we were flying, and I couldn't read a single sign in the place, you might assume we were in a shitty mega bus. Of course I would end up abducted by aliens and still have to take a mega bus. Fuck my luck.

I lean my head onto the window while the bus slows, as does the rest of the traffic until we come to a complete stop. We are flying through some alien city, the buildings tall enough to tower well above most of the traffic, but when I peer down, the ground is obscured by thick blue clouds...or maybe smog? Like I know jack shit about this world anyway.

Aliens of bizarre shapes and sizes crane their necks in their own ships to see what the hold up is. I swear I even hear a horn honk. I guess traffic is the same no matter the galaxy right? Well I mean, if there were four layers of traffic stacked on top of each other and cars all flew...

"Deenz don't have balls, or really any genitals at all, you know," Jessy says, as she settles back into her seat. "They're hive bred, and don't really give a dill about sex or us. That's probably why they're used to transport human women."

"Where are they taking us, and what the fuck kind of shot did that asshole just give me?" I ask.

"How about we start over, shall we?" she says, brushing her hair behind her ear. "Hi, I'm Jessy, what's your name?"

She holds out her hand to me. I take it, begrudgingly.

"Opal, my name's Opal. The last thing I remember is driving up to the lookout to eat my sushi after my shift at the Crafty Crab." I gesture around the strange bus. "And now I'm here, obviously not on Earth, and getting random needles shoved into my thigh by an asshole alien without genitals." I shake her hand with a big false smile.

"So you *are* new; you'll get used to it here. Dancing isn't so bad; you could have ended up in a brothel. At least the aliens can't touch us." Jessy sees my eyes widen in horror and tries to double back. "As long as you listen to the purple guys everything will be all right. We actually have pretty nice accommodations back on the station. Really, you could have done a lot worse."

"Great, I get a bunk house to share with all the other trafficked human women. Just what a little girl dreams of." I look into her dark green eyes and see a flash of compassion. "How long have you been here?"

"I'm not quite sure, but if I had to guess, two or three years? We don't really keep track."

"Oh...years...fabulous. So you've never tried to get away?" I ask, losing any hint of the sarcasm I first gave her. "I'm no dancer. What if I just wanted to go home?"

"Oh sweetie, no," she says, her voice actually attempting to be comforting this time. "Can I ask if you...did you have anyone at home? Family, maybe a boyfriend?" Jessy puts her hands over mine.

"Well, not really."

I think of my mom and dad who passed right after I left for college. Who knew carbon monoxide could ruin your whole life over the course of a night? A boyfriend? I don't know if I would call my Tinder hookups with adult men who lived in their parent's basements boyfriend material...

"Yeah, that's the common denominator for all of us here; we're unattached." She takes her hands back and crossed her arms over her chest again. "If you want to stick near me tonight, that's fine. I can show you the ropes. Dancing's not hard; it's even easier with the shot."

"Wait, you never told me what was in the shot."

"Think of it like an alien spanish fly, really gets us," Jessy throws up the sign for air quotes, "*dancing* if you know what I mean. But we're all in these plastic bubbles, so no one can touch. It's easy just to ignore the aliens. Plus, not all species are as unpleasant to look at as our Deenz captors."

"That asshole gave me a horny shot? What the fuck!" I slam

my fist against the plastic of the bench seat. I'm angry things are out of my control, but given the shit card I had been dealt on Earth, this kind of seems like a lateral move. Why the fuck am I not freaking out more? Maybe I'm in shock.

"Yes ma'am. We get our go-go juice about twenty minutes out from the club—I suggest just enjoying the ride. Although we normally don't hit traffic like this. This bus will get...interesting if the traffic doesn't pick up soon." She peeks her head around mine to try and see what the hold up is.

"Why don't we just fly over it?" I ask. I mean, wouldn't that be the benefit of flying versus driving?

"Well, we aren't flying for one, we're in a magnetic field, so we can't really leave it."

"How do you know that? Are you just really observant?"

Jessy chuckles. "You might not believe me, Opal, but I'm an honest-to-god rocket scientist...I got picked up outside of Cape Canaveral on my lunch break." She flips her hair to the other side of her head dramatically. "I think my hair is what got me picked up. The dancing isn't ideal, but part of me isn't too sad about getting to see what's out there, I suppose. All the girls who dance have something interesting going on physically. I mean check out those curves on you, girl!"

I try my best not to scoff, but she's right. I'm all tits and ass and had been using it to my advantage while serving at the Crafty Crab, stashing away all the tips I could to try and keep Mom and Dad's house from going into foreclosure. I guess there is no stopping the courts now. I'm not even sure how long I've been gone.

"Thanks. How far out are we from where we're going?"

"Oh, it's a club right on the beach. You can't see from here in the city but Sontafrul 6 is a beach planet. It's a huge tourist destination for other aliens. It's probably one of my favorites in our rotation."

Jessy seems earnest and honestly excited to get there. I hadn't had a vacation since my folks died; maybe a beach planet didn't sound so bad.

I shift in my seat and notice an annoying itch beginning in my crotch. I shift again, attempting to scratch the itch without my hands. The seam from my bandage-style bikini rolls over my clit, and I have to bite my lip to not let out an audible moan. Heaven help me if I don't try that move again. It feels good, better than it should—*Oh shit, the spanish fly.* I turn toward Jessy to make sure I hadn't tipped off what I was actually doing.

"Girl, you would be surprised what I can ignore. I heard our lovely purple overlord say he gave you extra, so do what you gotta do to take the edge off. We don't seem to be moving anytime soon," Jessy says as she settles in and closes her eyes.

I guess I hadn't been very discreet.

"You know, it's frowned upon to diddle yourself in front of new friends, or in public, or on a bus…" I laugh nervously as my nipples bead underneath the tight weave of my top. It's skimpy on the least endowed girls on the bus but on me it's downright pornographic.

"Opal, *you're new.* I've been getting these shots for years. The first few times are intense. Now I'm not gonna help you get off, so don't get any ideas; I draw the line there. But I can sure as shit turn my head if you need some personal time. Hell, the other girls had to do it for me when I was new too. Honestly, do what you need to, I swear I don't care." She works her shoulders into the molded plastic seat, and it looks like she's settling in for a nap.

Maybe I could ignore the damn shot. Did I want to be a feral mess on a bus in space? Fuck no. Did it seem like I had much of a choice? The way my pussy throbbed said no.

"Jessy, are you sure? I'm literally about to put my hands down my pants, so you need to say no if you're just joking or this is some weird hazing thing."

The bitch fakes a snore and turns away from me. Well, I guess this would make for a great game of Never Have I Ever one day.

Unfortunately, I am a visual gal, and I search the bus for something to inspire me. The purple son of a bitch who put me in this situation stares at me in disgust, his scales slick with whatever nastiness he's secreting.

That's never gonna happen. I turn my gaze outside the bus. The four rows of traffic have so many interesting vehicles, but most of the pilots leave a lot to be desired. I see a tall alien with some tentacles in a craft that looks like a cluster of clear pink bubbles. His face is very alien, unsettlingly so even, but maybe we could do something with those appendages, right? He'll have to do for now, because whatever is in that shot is sending all my blood away from my brain and straight to my crotch. I slide my hand down the stretchy blue bikini bottom and press my palm against my throbbing sex.

Fuck, I'm soaked.

I push my middle finger between my lips, sliding against my swollen clit—searching for friction. My free hand pulls down the top over my generous tit and I pluck at my nipple with my fingers. The oversensitive flesh sends sparks right down to my core. The bus shifts slightly as it groans for a few feet before stopping. As it moves, I slide two fingers lower. I stay near the opening of my pussy, circling the sensitive nerves near my entrance. Could tentacle daddy stuff me with one of his thick, pulsating tentacles? I've never been a tentacle porn girl but shit, desperate times call for desperate measures.

I open my eyes, expecting to see the slightly off-putting face of an alien I'd want to use just for his appendages, but instead stare directly into the eyes of someone else. The long sleek looking craft next to me holds a startlingly humanoid face. Sure his skin is smooth and gray, almost like shark skin, but his face is masculine and his nose is regal. His long muscular neck sits on even brawnier shoulders. Those shoulders are draped in a green suit of fabric. It's not a suit as I'm accustomed to on Earth, but it looks like formal wear of some kind to be sure.

The alien's eyes are deep set and blue, and they are boring

7

into me as I grind against my hand. Fuck, can an alien be hot? Because it could just be the damned shot, but he's fucking gorgeous. He blinks rapidly and swipes a large square hand over his gorgeous face and tucks his white hair behind his ear. His ear fans into a delicate frill where my cartilage would curve. As he tucks the short length of thick hair behind his ear, he traces a finger over a set of gills on his neck.

Gills? As if his otherworldly beauty didn't remind me he wasn't human, the gills sure as shit do.

I raise my chin to him, as if to say, "Yeah I see you watching me, you weird, sexy thing," and I swear I see him smirk.

That's just what I need. I replace tentacle daddy in my fantasy with hot shark guy and get to getting. By now, my finger is working my clit with pressure, and my orgasm builds. I wiggle my top all the way down and use my biceps to push my tits together. Will this get a response out of the handsome alien stranger? I lick my lips and push two fingers inside of my pussy again but deeper this time.

I don't know for sure if he has a dick, but I bet if he does it's as thick as the rest of him. I imagine shark guy bending me over the back of the seat in front of me and slamming his cock into me. With my tits pushed together and my hand deep inside of me I bite my lip. Fuck it feels good to be watched. How have I never done this before?

Hot alien guy's breath fogs up the window and his smile broadens. I feel the buzz of my translator chip as his mouth moves. I can't hear what he's saying but somehow my brain knows…maybe the chip works visually and auditorily? I'm not going to overthink it, because he's saying things I want to hear.

"Are you enjoying yourself, little human?" my mind translates—I wish I could hear his voice, I'm sure it would be as sexy as the rest of him.

"You're so fucking hot." My ass and legs clench with the kinetic energy of my building orgasm. The alien throws back his head slightly and a roar of laughter fills his whole chest.

"Do I inspire this display then?" So he must have a translator chip too.

"You're certainly going to be the one that finishes it," I say. "What would you do if you could touch me right now?"

He licks his fucking perfect full lips. "I'd want to taste you, run my tongue up that neat little human cunt of yours. I'd let you ride my face until you took everything you needed from me."

His throat bobs as his hand drifts below the window frame toward his lap. Sit on his face? Maybe I'm too far away, and he can't see how ample this ass actually is.

"I wouldn't want to smother you, sugar, but the thought is appreciated."

The handsome stranger pauses and moves his lips before my translation device catches up.

"I assure you, little human, that my body can handle you sitting that glorious ass right here. You could stay as long as you want, I can get plenty of air from these," he says as he points to his gills.

Well fuck. My clit is almost too sensitive at this point, and I switch to sliding my fingers down the sides of it. Ride the handsome alien's face? I want to close my eyes and imagine grinding over that gorgeous chin. I want to sink my hands in that pale hair of his and hold on as he licks me to completion. I want to have his tongue work long slow licks over my swollen clit. I don't want to miss anything he says though, so I keep my eyes open and my focus on him.

"I'm close," I say. "I wish you could touch me."

"What's your name, little human?" he asks.

I hesitate for a moment, but realize given the circumstances I've found myself in, telling a hot stranger my name is the least of my worries. "Opal."

"Opal, do you want to come for me?" His mouth slowly smiles as he speaks.

"Fuck yes."

☆KE'AIN

"Think of your hand as mine." I have no idea what planets have aligned to have this goddess on display next to me, but if the wars have taught me anything it's to enjoy the good times while they're here. And goddess help me, Opal is stunning.

I haven't frequented many of the clubs that provide human entertainment. My position doesn't allow for breaches in etiquette that might allow me such fun, although I have seen quite a few human women on the satellite signals picked up from their planet. The human mating videos always show women with lean bodies, and their breasts, while large, seem hard and set.

Opal's body is all wonderful softness. As she rubs furiously under her thermal bandages, her plentiful tits bounce, and I know that if she was spread bare before me I would worship that beautiful ass. I want to pull that curved pink body into mine and pound my cock into her cunt until she screams my name.

I flip a switch on the console next to me, alerting my driver that I don't wish to be disturbed. My hand has been working my cock through the cloth of my clothing long enough to be painfully hard. I press my waistband button and the fabric opens automatically. I work the bead of precum from my cock's tip down its length, imagining her pillowy lips might be there instead.

Opal, with her perfect soft tits, keeps her eyes on me. She's arching against the orange plastic seat and I see her hand working frantically. I fist my cock as I know I could have her already coming under me. I would wring every last drop from her orgasm, this sweet little human.

"Would you be able to take my cock, Opal?" I ask her honestly. She's so tiny compared to my species, the Fil'ens. I worry that I might be too large for her. "I want so very much for you to take all of it into that soft body of yours."

Opal's chest rises and falls rapidly with the pace of her

breathing. She cocks her head as she moves her hand from the waistband of her thermal bandages and brings two fingers to her mouth.

"I'm no quitter," she says as she adds a third finger to her mouth and slicks them with her spit. She runs them down her soft belly slowly before driving them back into her sex. I see the wetness from her cunt darken the thermal bandages, and I want to rip them off her body. My cock jerks as I watch Opal push her shoulders into the seat as her legs and core tighten. She keeps her eyes locked on me.

"I would fill you up so tight," I say as I work my hand. "I'd want you to milk every last drop from this cock".

Opal's body is taut like a bow, and she keeps her dilated eyes on me the entire time. Her lips are swollen and her face is flushed that same strange red color as the skin over her nipples is. I would kill to suck one of those hardened tips into my mouth.

My own hand works the head of my cock quickly as I tell the beauty before me, "Come for me, Opal".

As she does, she finally closes her eyes and rides out the wave of her pleasure. She is a goddess and I'm just her suppli-cant. I give my cock two more rough tugs before finding my own release. I don't close my eyes though, my pleasure is coming from the vision in front of me—she is carnal perfection.

Opal pushes the mass of blonde curls back from her face, sticky with sweat, and turns her face to mine just as traffic begins to move again. She puts a palm up to the window as she realizes her transport unit is pulling away from my cruiser.

"What's your name?" she asks, her breath fogging up the glass of her window.

I don't have time to respond before her lane of traffic moves ahead of mine. I want nothing more than to hear my name on her lips. I can't help but feel a pang in my heart at the loss of such beauty as she pulls away. I wipe my hand on a cloth from the bar next to me and grab my data pad to write down the name plastered on the side of Opal's transport unit. I buzz the communication button, and the gruff voice of my driver acknowledges me.

"Follow the human transport unit, send the royal attorney our coordinates, and have him meet us wherever they stop."

Next time I'm going to taste Opal's release for myself.

CHAPTER 2
☆SPACE
LEGALITIES☆

☆KE'AIN

MY COMMUNICATOR BUZZES for the tenth time this past hour as I click a button to ignore the call once more. The royal attaché, and my personal butler, is an incessant man, but I really don't want to have to come up with a pleasant lie to tell him.

Why aren't you at the ribbon cutting for the new magtrain? he would ask.

Well, sorry Al'frind, my hand found its way to my cock after seeing an off-world beauty in a traffic jam. Yeah, probably best to keep this bit to myself for at least the foreseeable future.

Was it absurd that I made my driver follow the human entertainer bus? In retrospect probably. Was I a man possessed with nothing but thoughts of Opal's soft human body still? Entirely.

I watched out the window as the high-rises of downtown give way to the beaches my planet is famous for. The universe's tourists have driven our GDP up to the point where my family, the rulers of Sontafrul 6, are some of the richest beings in the galaxy. There are times the money is nice, like now as I wait

to our destination. Where I would have the
pay any cost needed to acquire Opal.

rest of the time, the money and the title I bore suffo-
ne. The endless parade of eligible women my parents place
in front of me make me want nothing more than to renounce
myself as heir. The princesses and diplomats from off world are
chosen specifically for what alliances or capital they might bring
to our dynasty.

They are insufferable, haughty and stuck up from a lifetime
of grooming. I am the end goal for years of etiquette classes: a
handsome and wealthy prince who could bring more prestige to
their own families. I am a trophy.

If they only knew that I would give everything to have them
all go away, to leave the Fi'len people alone. To be able to tear
down the high-rises, the casinos, the hotels. To ban the cruise
ships from our oceans. To have my planet back, to live simply
like when I was a boy. I'd give it all up.

The outlanders take my planet's natural splendor, use it for
their vacations, polluting our air and water in the process, and
go home without giving it a second thought. They take and take
and take. And for what? Credits? I'd give it all up.

I laugh to myself, realizing that I'd give it all up after I obtain
Opal.

Obtain.

I'm as bad as the outlanders. She's a person, not an object. I'll
do my best to convince her to come with me. I will make Opal
mine. But remembering her once more, could I blame myself for
thinking with my cock? She'll want to come with me, won't she?
After the display in the traffic jam, I should have no doubts.

My cruiser slows outside of The Gem, the most popular club
for outlander tourists in all of Sontafrul 6. It does look like a
jewel, the pink glass building nestled on a black sand beach and
our ocean's teal waters lapping softly at the shore. Rows and
rows of tourists line the veranda overlooking the ocean. Cock-
tails grace the "hands" of every conceivable shape. The faces of

the guests flash with excitement as Opal's transport unit pulls up. I wonder how many people have come to see the human women tonight?

Humans are rare outside of their home planet. The UGS, the Universal Governing Senate, decreed Earth a hazardous nature preserve. Very few beings are allowed to enter Earth's airspace, and even fewer are allowed to take humans off world. This solves two issues. One, because of their sexually compatible bodies, humans were often trafficked throughout the universe against their will. Two, they carry viruses only seen on Earth, and without proper decontamination practices they'd end up wiping out entire species.

I think of Opal. *She doesn't seem like a world killer.*

Since the ruling, all humans brought off world do so through a strict application process. I've heard that there's waiting lists over a decade long to join the entertainment companies. They're one of the few organizations with enough money to foot the permit bills. Opal must have shone brightly above all the other applicants. How could she not? The image of her body is burned into my psyche. Without her in my field of vision, I feel empty.

It takes every ounce of willpower in me to not dash from the car as my driver pulls up to the front of The Gem. To run and scoop up Opal's soft pink body as she exits the bus. Seeing Gra'eth's dour face as he stands on the steps of The Gem's entrance helps me contain my excitement. The royal attorney looks positively pissed.

As my driver opens the door, I hear the click of the tourists' data pads. *Great, photos.* I'm sure by early morning the tabloids would have articles up on the network that I would have to explain somehow to my parents. All the more reason to get this done quickly.

"What in f'tee am I doing at a club this late, Ke'ain?" His arms are crossed against his broad chest as he complains.

Ah, Gra'eth. You might say he's the closest thing I have to a best friend. He was one of the few younglings allowed around me as I grew up. Seeing as he's always been a bit of a buzzkill, royal attorney is the perfect position for him. Even though he loves nothing more than to give me a hard time, I know that he'll always find a way to help me if I truly need him.

"Good to see you too Gra'eth!" I smile broadly and hug him with one arm as is customary with our people. I point one of my four fingers toward the human transport unit. "We're going to grease whatever wheels are needed so that I can bring Opal back to the palace with me."

"What in goddesses' names is an Opal?" He taps his translator chip as if he misunderstood the translation, and his brow knit in confusion. "If you want precious stones you have plenty at home Ke'ain."

"Opal is a human woman. She's coming back with us tonight, no exceptions." I keep my smile up as her face flashes across my mind.

Gra'eth's lively gray color drains from his face as he blanches to a sickly white. "A human? F'tee Ke'ain! Those things are riddled with diseases. Where the f'tee did you even meet a human woman?"

My poor flustered friend has well... issues with germs, to say the least.

"Gra'eth, you know as well as I do that if she's come off Earth there's been a lengthy decontamination process. I assure you she's clean," I say, clamping my hand onto his shoulder as I lead him toward her transport unit. "As far as where I met her, well that would be in the traffic jam right before my driver called you." I wink at him.

Gra'eth rolls his eyes, "Oh, so you lost all sense of reason because the blood drained to your other head?" He sighs. "I've got some satellite transmissions I can lend you if you've just got a human scratch you need to itch."

I try not to let the comment bother me, but my hand pinches a bit tighter on his shoulder.

"You misunderstand Gra'eth, *she is mine*," I growl.

His eyes widen in shock. "A human entertainer is your mate?"

Mate. The word holds meaning for my people. Is Opal my mate? I've never felt a tug as strong as this before. Not for the glorified dolls that are brought before me, not for the flings with palace staff my parents try their best to keep under wraps.

"I'm...not sure," I say, "but I know I'm not leaving here without her." I release my grip as we get close enough to the transport unit to see the human women begin to disembark. My friends' eyes go thoughtful for a moment, and then I see the determination behind them.

"Well, until you're sure I guess we can't let this Opal out of our sight can we?" He resigns himself to help me.

"No, I can't, can I?"

We both watch as human women from shades of rich browns to the palest ivory disembark their vehicle. Each woman steps from the transport unit into a clear security pod. For humans to be as rare as they are, the entertainment company surely wants to make sure they stay safe. The pods float in a line toward the side entrance of The Gem as they queue up for the performance. Human dancing is supposed to be some of the most erotic in the universe, at least if you believe the slogan plastered on the side of their transport.

After my experience with Opal, I just might believe it.

"F'tee... is that her?"

Gra'eth's breath catches, and I'm about to knock into the side of his jaw with my fist. *Did I not just say she was mine?* But as I see the flash of red hair climb into her security pod, I calm my boiling blood.

"No, my Opal is one thousand times more beautiful than that silly human."

"You must be mistaken friend," he says, dazed.

I ignore his comment, because that's when I see her. Opal's curved body, her thermal bandages still wet from our earlier experience. Right before she steps into the security pod, I can even smell her. She smells sweeter than any ambrosia I've ever encountered. My palms begin to sweat and my cock to twitch as I'm finally reunited with Opal. I begin to walk her direction when I feel Gra'eth's hand on my chest.

"Patience Ke'ain. They're late for their performance. Now might not be the best time to broach the subject. Let's wait until after, and we can bring the Deenz and Opal into a private room for an agreement to be made. Even if she does want to come with you, I'm sure her contract with the company will need to be bought out," he says tactfully.

I watch as Opal taps on the plastic of her security pod. Her face seems... worried.

"Private room now. I'll pay for whatever the fee is. She can perform for me alone." My tone lets Gra'eth know it's a royal order, not a request. He sighs and makes his way over to the Deenz, already transferring credits with his data pad.

The club owner, a fellow Fil'en, quickly leads me through the frustrating clicks of tourist photos to a back room. He pushes aside a heavy curtain, and we enter the room. The space is draped in swaths of dark green velvet, and a large ottoman sits in the middle of the room. A fully stocked bar with an android attendant is ready to make me whatever cocktail I desire.

"Your Highness, if you would have told us of your visit sooner, I would have been able to avoid all the photos. I am so sorry we were not properly prepared for your visit." The owner bows deeply. "I hope our service can make up for that fact going forward. Please let me know if there's anything you require".

He keeps the deep bow until I wave him off impatiently. How long does it take a damn security pod to get from the door to this room? I tap my feet, agitated.

"Welcome, Your Highness." The android's digital voice fills

the space. "Might I offer you our finest thr'uik cocktail to start your evening?" He cocks his head, miming genuine emotions.

I nod; a cocktail might calm my nerves a bit. His metal arms work at record speed, cutting fruit and pouring the top shelf liquor. When he hands me the delicate glass, I down it in a single sip. Unfortunately, I'm still on edge.

When the curtain at the entrance sweeps back and I see her pod float into the room, my breath catches. Opal is here. She peeks around the room nervously before her eyes settle on me and a smirk spreads across her face. Everything about her is just so pink and nubile. I look down at my own gray skin and wonder if she finds it as pleasing as I do hers.

"Sharkboy!" she yells. "I didn't think I'd see you again".

Her voice is amplified through the security pod's speaker. It's low and lovely, though the accent isn't one I've heard before . She draws out her vowels and drops some of the harder consonants of the human language.

"Sharkboy?" I ask, confused. Flashes of vicious ocean predators are brought to my mind by my translator chip. "I am not a shark Opal, I am Ke'ain. I am of the Fil'en". I puff up my chest, proud of my people.

"I know you're not a shark darlin', your skin just reminds me of one," she says. "I don't have a whole lot of alien experience, you'll have to forgive me."

Forgive her, for what offense? I'm overjoyed I can be here with her again, despite the separation the pod might cause. I drop to my knees, so that our eyes are level.

"You have nothing to apologize for," I say as I place my hand on the plastic barrier that separates us. Opal looks thoughtfully at my hand and places hers up to mirror my own.

"You sure are pretty on your knees, Ke'ain," she breathes.

Even though her accent butchers the proper pronunciation of my name I am filled with joy. I look into her beautiful brown eyes and see that when they look at my face they dilate in pleasure. Her nipples peak through the fabric of her thermal bandages again. *She wants me.*

"So do you think I have an extra finger, or are you missing one?" She giggles as she points out our small differences.

"It must be me who is at fault, for I've never seen anything as perfect as you." My breath fogs up the plastic.

"Oh..." she says shyly, "well, the purple guy told me you wanted a private dance?"

Where is my bold Opal from before?

"If you so wish it Opal, I promise not to do anything you don't want to do."

"Well, you paid for it, but promise you won't laugh—I've never done this before." Doubt crosses her face.

"Is this your first night with the company?" I inquire.

"Ha, yeah, you could say that." She moves her hand back and though a little unsteady, begins to sway her hips. "Is this okay?"

Okay? I watch her hips sway back and forth. I am mesmerized as she traces her hand up the soft curve of her tummy. She opens her legs and pushes her hand up against the plump mound of her sex that is under the thermal bandages. Her breathing speeds up and she flashes a nervous smile toward me.

"God, I'm sorry I'm so bad at this," she says, dropping to her knees in defeat.

"Opal, you could sit there and read aloud math equations and you'd still have my full attention," I coo. I want to stroke those blonde waves on her head. I want to smell her again.

"You're nice, Ke'ain. I didn't think aliens would be nice." She frowns.

"Why would you come here then? If you don't like dancing and you thought all other species would be cruel?" I'm confused why any human woman would go through the rigorous application process if her whole heart wasn't in it?

Opal balks. "You think I wanted to leave Ear—"

We both turn our heads as the curtain opens and Gra'eth and the Deenz wait for my approval to enter. I wave them in.

"Prince Ke'ain," the Deenz speaks, and Opal's mouth drops upon hearing my title, "my hive is honored that you would grace us with your patronage for our lowly company. I hope that the human woman is providing sufficient entertainment?"

"She is perfect," I say. "Did Gra'eth come to an agreement for Opal's contract? As long as she accepts the terms?"

"The royal attorney was more than generous in his offerings. You are a kind and fair ruler," the Deenz responds, dipping into a bow.

I turn back to see Opal's confused face take in the scene outside her security pod. I place my hand back on the plastic.

"If you want to, you could come back with me," I say.

Opal knits her brows together. "Do I have to dance anymore? What about the shots?"

I don't know what shots she speaks of but I make my promise to her. "You will do nothing you don't readily want to."

Opal shrugs, sighing as if resigned, and gestures to the thermal bandages. "Get me some clothes that cover more than this, and I'll go wherever you want me to."

Her acceptance of my offer is not the jubilant response I wanted, but I'll take it all the same.

"Open the security pod," I tell the Deenz.

He pops open his data pad and begins to input the passcode to unlock its door.

"Wait, wait, wait... I agreed to obtain the human for you, Prince Ke'ain, but please for the love of the goddess, let me process her through decontamination—I already have enough explaining to do to your parents. Let me promise them I did my due diligence for your safety," Gra'eth pleads with me.

"Fine," I say begrudgingly before turning back to Opal. "Only a short while until I can feel your hand in mine, sweet creature".

Her eyes seem far off for a second, but then she turns to

Gra'eth and speaks. "I'm not a stray dog asshole, I'm perfectly clean."

She has fire inside of her, this human.

Gra'eth grimaces before flipping open his communicator. "Send a private decon team to Prince Ke'ain's estate. We've got an incoming package in thirty clicks".

I look back at the pissed, confused, and still somehow aroused Opal.

Mine.

CHAPTER 3
☆YOU SAID NO SHOTS☆

☆KE'AIN

THE GUARDS LIFT the security pod into a palace transport unit as Opal runs her hands up and down her breasts. Even without an audience it seems that human women are insatiable. She squeezes her thighs together and places her hands on the plastic of the pod as our eyes find each other.

"Soon, little human," I say with a smile. I get back into my cruiser and settle in for the hour commute to the palace.

———————

I push at the hard plastic walls now quarantining off the study of my palace apartment. To my right, Gra'eth looks pleased at the sterility of it all, but I'm frustrated to have agreed to this second round of decontamination for Opal. I know she hates the idea after her stray dog remark to Gra'eth, but I also know he's right. Opal will be a hard enough sell as a palace guest to my parents after these safety measures. I don't want to make it any harder for her here since she trusted me enough to want to stay.

My face perks up as I see guards lead her security pod into

the clean room. I raise my hand and suddenly feel like a lovesick fool as she frowns in my direction.

"Ke'ain, I fear you're coming across as *overeager* to your guest. Why don't you check with the staff that her quarters are ready, make yourself useful?" Gra'eth grouses.

"Gra'eth, one day I can't wait to see what kind of creature brings you to your knees. If you think for a second I'm leaving her alone, her *first* night in the palace, you might be even stupider than I thought." As I speak the royal attorney rolls his eyes at me.

Once Opal's security pod is zipped up in the temporary clean room, the decon techs enter the passcode into a data pad, and one holds out a hand to help her step down. It takes everything in me to hold back the snarl that rises in my throat as I see his gloved hand slip into hers. Opal looks back toward me, her pupils entirely constricted, and her face is blanched.

"Opal, it'll be alright," I tell the obviously frightened human. "Humans just can carry certain viruses that many alien bodies can't handle. I had to agree to this to bring you here."

She relaxes a little as the decon tech guides her to the metal table where she sits her beautiful ass. I find myself wishing my face was her preferred seat instead. I swipe my hand over my eyes in an attempt to clear my head.

The two techs spray her down with an atomized sanitizer. She coughs slightly and sticks out her tongue, her body retching at its chemical taste. One tech behind Opal uses surgical scissors to cut away at the thermal bandages wrapped around her breasts. She wheels around and smacks him on the side of his face with force I didn't think she was capable of. I hear him shout in surprise, and he brings a gloved hand up to the hazmat suit covering his face.

"What the fuck are you doing?" she barks.

The tech looks toward me with wide eyes.

"Tell her we need to remove the thermal bandages to properly decontaminate her," he says.

"I can understand, you asshole. Did you ever think maybe you should ask me before stripping me naked?" Opal's jaw is set into a scowl.

"Please let Opal know what you're doing going forward," I tell the techs. "Opal, they do have to remove them."

Opal's frown deepens. "Can you at least give me some privacy then?"

Although my mind flashes back to her very public display on the bus, I do the right thing and nod. I pull Gra'eth into the dining room even though privacy seems laughable to imagine between us now. I barely have time to sit down at the table before I hear her human scream. My stomach drops as the noise causes my brain to panic.

"F'tee privacy," I tell Gra'eth as I run back into the room.

There Opal stands, in nothing but her beautiful pink skin. She's holding the surgical scissors in her hand, jabbing at the two decon techs who are holding up their arms up in compliance. One tech holds a syringe in his raised palm.

"Eyes to the fucking floor, Gra'eth."

He drops his gaze from my naked Opal. It's bad enough I have to allow the techs to touch her. I won't suffer Gra'eth looking upon what I know is *mine*.

"You are not sticking me with that fucking needle you alien nerd!" she bellows. She turns toward me, her sad eyes in opposition to her vexed mouth. "You said no fucking shots."

I look toward Gra'eth who stares dutifully at his shoes. "I did give her my word."

He taps his fingers over his crossed arms, screwing his mouth to the side in thought. "You did, and what good is a prince if his word means nothing?"

He pulls his data pad from his breast pocket and types. His eyebrows rise as he reads.

"We could test her for the specific bacteria and viruses instead, but there's a twelve hour lead time on results," he states matter of factly.

"Have staff bring the bed here," I say. "Opal, we'll need to have you sleep here for just tonight, is that alright?"

"No shots?" she asks.

"No shots...just promise not to hurt the decon techs. They need to grab a few swabs and we'll test you first instead of treating you preventively."

"Where do they need to swab?" she asks, eyeing the wary techs.

"Yes Gra'eth, where *do* they need to swab?"

He shuffles his feet a bit and clears his throat. "Well, just the standard mucus membranes."

Opal cackles maniacally with the scissors still raised. "Great, so a fucking shot or a pussy swab?"

"Well, don't forget," he taps his data pad again, "nose, eyes, and throat as well, at least that's the extent of it for humans... I think?" He scrolls on his data pad, his human research obviously being done on the fly.

I frown. Opal is obviously displeased with her two choices. "Yes, but I promise it will all be easier after we can make sure you won't get anyone sick."

As we look into each other's eyes, I see some of the tension leave her body. She drops the scissors to the floor, the stainless steel clanking on marble, with a look of defeat on her face. As if she suddenly realizes that she's standing there bare for the world to see, her pink skin flushes red, and she covers herself with her hands.

"I'll do the swabs, just please let me do it without y'all watching." She stares at the floor, no longer meeting my eyes.

"Of course, Opal. I'm sorry this has been so incredibly invasive. I wish there was another way." I nod to her but have to stop myself from dropping into a bow. I can only imagine what protocol that would breach. "Is there anything I can have brought to you? Are you hungry, thirsty, perhaps a screen?"

She looks at me and sighs. "I'm fine."

I make it a point to pull Gra'eth toward the doorway. I'll give Opal the privacy she wants.

"Actually," she says, "if you have a book, something in English, that might be nice."

I turn back to her, pulling Gra'eth's elbow as he swivels back to face her with me.

"Of course, I'll find something immediately. Good night Opal," I say before turning back toward Gra'eth and seeing him looking toward the clean room—looking at Opal.

I tighten my grip on his arm and drag him quickly into the adjoining room. "If you ever look at Opal in this state of undress again, I will pluck those stupid eyeballs from your thick skull."

Gra'eth gulps at my intensity.

"Watch where you put your fucking hand!" I hear my precious little human order at the techs.

"Ke'ain... aren't humans supposed to be well... more compliant than yours seems right now?"

I'll admit to myself that yes, this Opal seems different from the one from a few hours ago. Every story I've ever heard on her species has been about how obedient and overtly sexual they are —it makes them perfect performers to travel the universe.

"Put yourself in her position, Gra'eth! She's away from her home planet for the first time, this was her first night on the job, and now she's been whisked into the royal palace and has been poked and prodded beyond common decency." I walk over to the bar and pour myself a stiff drink.

"I guess you're right," he sighs.

"Oh, and pull whatever strings you need to acquire a human book for her, tonight."

"Ke'ain, where in the f'tee am I supposed to find a human book at this hour?"

"That seems a whole lot like your problem, and not mine." I sip from my glass and let the thr'uik liquor warm my chest.

Gra'eth pushes himself up from the table, slipping his data

pad back into the breast pocket of his suit. "Well, I suppose sleep is out of the question for me tonight?"

I chuckle under my breath as he leaves. Sleep. I won't be able to sleep again until Opal lies in my bed next to me. I hear the slap of a human palm against the plastic of a hazmat suit.

"Jesus Christ, is there a brain in that big head of yours?" My little human's angry voice echoes from the study. "I said watch your fucking hands!"

Part of me worries for her, but I'll give her the privacy she requests. A larger part of me worries more for the decon techs. I flip open my data pad and leave a note for the royal accountant to double their invoice fee.

I worry just for a second that I'm in over my head with Opal, that I might have been thinking with my cock as Gra'eth suggested. I think of her pink face and know that it's not just my cock though. My chest fills with pressure as I clasp my four fingers over my sternum.

The little human makes my heart want to explode.

CHAPTER 4
☆THE PANIC ROOM☆

☆OPAL

HE THINKS I can't see him just in the other room, but his long legs are draped over the side of the chair, and I can see the tips of his gray toes through the doorway. I sit in the plush bed and smooth the wrinkles of my green dress. It's cut for someone much taller than me, and I'm a little bit swamped by its proportions—but it's so much better than the bikini. I wish I could be madder at Ke'ain after the humiliation of my decontamination, but I'm glad I don't have to dance in that damn bubble anymore —even if I'm scared of what being here might mean. What does Ke'ain expect after what the fucking shot had me showing him just hours before?

I sit up when a door creaks open. Ke'ain's friend, or maybe his assistant, walks by the plastic walls of my temporary room. He doesn't make eye contact with me or acknowledge me, which is more than a little dehumanizing. He makes his way to stand in front of Ke'ain, clearing his throat as he pulls something small and rectangular from his breast pocket.

"Ke'ain…" I don't see my rescuer's feet move, and I think I

might even hear a soft snoring. "Ke'ain! For goddess's sake just get the f'tee up!" He knees his toe and Ke'ain inhales sharply.

"I'm up, I'm up…" He stands and shakes the sleep from his limbs. "What's the emergency Gra'eth?"

Gra'eth snorts. "The emergency was the errand you sent me on in the middle of the night, for the damn human book."

He tosses a worn paperback at his chest angrily. Ke'ain catches it deftly with his four fingered hand.

"Glad to see at least one of us is getting some sleep…" Gra'eth grumbles as he makes his way past me again.

When I turn back I see Ke'ain smiling in the doorway. He leans his muscular body against the door frame. He holds up the paperback like it's a prize pig, his face smug with pride.

"The book, Opal, has been acquired."

"Well, look at you. At least I'll have something to make the time go by a bit more quickly, won't I darlin'?" I say. "What's the title?"

Ke'ain's face drops into a frown. "I'm not too well versed in any of the written languages of Earth, so I'm afraid you'll have to let me know what the title is."

Ke'ain walks toward me, and as he does, he nearly trips over the tubing that runs out the window. I assume it supplies my little quarantine station with clean air from outdoors. He tries to conceal his stumble as he straightens out the leg of his suit when his body is pitched forward, and I can't help but laugh a bit at his expense. He ignores me, with an air of dignity, and presses the paperback up against the plastic wall.

I tilt my head—the book is upside down—and read the title aloud to him, "Oh…it's *Lady Chatterley's Lover*."

Ke'ain looks at my tilted head, frowns, and slowly turns the book rightside up. "Is it not a good one?"

"I mean, I think it's good, so to speak…"

"What's it about?" my big alien asks.

"Well, I haven't read it, but it's"—wow, I guess that shot

bolstered my confidence more than I realized—"it's..." I cough as I say the last word, "erotic."

Ke'ains face pulses blue before he cracks into a chest splitting laugh. "It's what we've got tonight, little Opal. Do you want me to toss it out then?"

"No, no, no—I suppose it's better than nothing."

"Alright, let me just..." He reaches for the doorway before scratching his head. "I don't have a hazmat suit. I probably shouldn't..."

"It's alright, I should probably get some sleep anyway." I resign myself to a night alone without any entertainment.

"I could hold it up for you to read if you want. I don't mind at all—"

"Don't be silly, go get some sleep too. It's fine. It wasn't really on my to-read list, even though I do appreciate the thought." I start to shoo him off but I get distracted by the thick fog that begins to roll in through my airflow pipes. The purple smoke curls up the walls of my clean room.

"What's that?" Ke'ain asks dumbfounded.

"Um, why the fuck would I know?" I start to panic as the fog rises and the acrid taste of the gas hits my nose. I rush to cover my mouth and run to the locked plastic door before pausing at the keycode panel. I cough, trying desperately to not take in any more of the gas. "Ke'ain, what's the code?"

I swivel as I hear a thud against the plastic wall behind me. Ke'ain slams his muscular shoulder into the plastic barrier, and small cracks form as he repeats the previous motion.

"Ke'ain, just open the damn door!" The gas burns my lungs. I start to panic as my air is cut off and I choke. My lungs are desperate for fresh air.

He slams his shoulder against the crack again. "I don't—" he grunts, pushing his hulking frame against the crack "—know the damn—" until finally his shoulder comes crashing through the crack as the wall gives "—code!"

His body comes crashing to the floor along with shards of thick plastic. Air rushes into my clean room, and I take a gulping breath. It dulls the burning slightly, but I rush toward the fallen Ke'ain and try to lift his large frame from the floor. He pushes his long gray arms, pops his body up athletically, and wraps his arms around my frame. He rushes us both out through the smashed plexiglass.

The ease with which he lifts my body startles me, and he presses my face against his chest. His huge hand cradles me more gently than seems possible. He coughs, and turns his head, trying not to spit directly on me. I can't see where we're going, but I feel the percussion of his feet as they pound on the marble floor. The hinges of a door screech at the speed at which he flings it open.

Ke'ain lays me gently on something soft. A bed? I clear the fog from my eyes and cover my mouth as I can't stop the burning in my throat. Ke'ain slams his large hand onto a silver button next to the open door frame. With a whoosh, metal barriers roll up from the ceiling to floor, blocking off the door frame and window. The silver metal is almost corrugated in texture. It rolls over the ceiling and all the planes of metal meet; they slam shut with a clank.

"What in the world..." I say as I stare at the shiny silver that surrounds us.

The metallic surfaces shift to a forest scene, sunlight streaming through pink alien trees, with the soft hums of things that almost sound like crickets. Ke'ain slumps on the bed next to me, clearing his throat and rubbing his watering eyes...

"It's a panic room, developed to be soothing." He hacks a cough away from me before turning his hands to clasp my face. "Are you hurt?"

His eyes are wide and his face is full of fear. He looks up and down my body, as he waits for a response.

"I think I'm alright, Ke'ain..." I cough again, tilting my head down and putting my forehead on his chest. "I'm guessing that's not part of my decontamination process?"

He wraps his arms around me, and I allow myself to slump into his warm body. His skin feels like smooth leather, and it's strangely comforting. I push my body further into his, my eyelids heavy.

"No, I'm afraid it might be an assassination attempt." He pulls me up to sit, his blue eyes staring into mine. "I need you to stay awake, sweet Opal."

He pats my cheek, attempting to keep my eyes from closing. I know that his attempts are in vain. I can already feel my neck collapsing—I can't support my head. Taking one final gulp of air before my consciousness slips, I slump against Ke'ain's chest, my nose smooshing against his soft gray skin.

"You smell nice," are the last words I'm able to get out before the blackness takes over.

———

The sounds of the forest fill my ears as I crack my eyes open just the slightest bit. My head is heavy, and I am slumping against something warm, hard… and breathing?

My eyes fill with a blurred field of mottled gray and white. Whatever I'm resting up against smells like cedar and ocean spray. I shake the fog from my brain just enough to push against the warm thing and finally realize that I'm pushing against a chest. Its broad shoulders strain the fabric of the green shirt, the buttons open almost to its navel.

I tilt my head up and take in a strong jaw and closed eyes. I stroke the back of my hand across his burnished and highly arched cheekbones. His skin is so much smoother than mine. The head attached to the chest is a handsome one. As I sit up, I'm finally able to assess the angle at which my body has fallen.

I'm straddling the handsome gray man. He's a stranger…but why in the world would I be sitting on top of a stranger? Wait… who am I even?

I shift my hips slightly in an attempt to dismount the huge form from beneath me.

The gray man groans. Dragging my green dress up past my belly, he puts his four fingered hands onto my bare hips and pulls me deeper against him.

"What are you doing?" I ask, batting at his well-defined chest, hard enough to get the stranger's attention but not hard enough for him to toss me. I won't pretend his hardening crotch doesn't feel good grinding against my quickly heating core. The gray man peeks open one eyelid, and a puzzled look flashes across his features.

"Who, might I ask, are you?" He sounds curious and not at all angry, but I doubt he could be angry as he arches his hips up toward mine. "You know I don't even care who you are, as long as you stay right there for me."

His fingers dig deeper into my ample hips as he searches for more friction between us.

"Well, that's probably a good thing," I squeak out as I feel my pussy slicken. I press my hands against his chest and watch the gray man bite his lip. "Who are you?"

"I..." He unfortunately stops the movement of his hips and confusion knits his brows. "I don't know."

My eyes drift up. A strange forest of pink trees surrounds us, the light filtering through their translucent leaves. But the bedroom furniture seems too ornate just to be placed in a forest.

"So neither of us knows who we are," I look into his blue eyes, "and here we are, in bed, in the woods?"

Sitting up, moving his hands from my hips, then wraps his arms around my waist. The man is taller than I thought, his chin able to rest easily on top of my head. He moves his hands under my ass as he scoots to the edge of the bed and smoothly stands. I feel a little stupid, like a barnacle stuck to something beautiful, but the worry in my chest keeps me clinging tight to his form.

"I don't know what's happened, but maybe we should stick together until we figure it out." He paces toward the treeline.

"This is me sticking to you, literally," I guffaw nervously. "So, no issues there."

The man squeezes my ass in what I assume is supposed to be a comforting touch. Maybe we do know each other because his touch *is* comforting, among other things. His elbow hits something hard as he turns, and the image of trees and sun fizzes with static around the contact area. We realize the forest isn't real.

"We're not in the forest, little thing," he says. "We are in a box of some sort."

He shifts me to his hip and runs his free hand against the screens as he marks the perimeter of our enclosure. As he gets to the far end, he notices a silver box. With a flip of his thumb, he unlatches the lid and reveals a silver button.

"Do we press it?" I ask, craning my neck around him to look at the dubious little button.

"I don't think we have another choice, do we?" He steps back, shielding my body from the button before he reaches toward it. "Do I have your consent to push it?"

"Um, sure, I mean, if you think it's a good idea."

I grip his body harder as he presses the shiny chrome button. He brings his hand back quickly and guards my head, as if I'm the most precious cargo in the world. A gentle digital voice fills the room.

"Panic room stable, oxygen levels and environmental factors appropriate for both fi'len and human occupants. No active intruder found, palace currently intact. Two hours of the twelve-hour time delay remain until doors unlock. Rations can be dispersed by depressing button for five seconds."

The voice is gone as quickly as it arrives.

"We were passed out for *ten hours*?" I ask incredulously.

"It appears as though we have another two hours before we're released as well," he says, sitting on the edge of the bed, shifting my body with ease once again to straddle him.

"We must know each other, right? Maybe something happened to our memories. Is that even possible?"

"There are many parts of myself that feel like they know you, that know your body at least." He winks.

It must be true though, because that statement coming from someone I didn't know would put me on edge, wouldn't it?

"Do you think we're in danger?"

"I think it's safe to say we're in some kind of predicament, that is sure." He looks back thoughtfully to the silver button floating in the screens of forest. "It appears we'll be here for another two hours no matter the outcome, though." He searches my face and stares down at his own hands as they clasp around my waist.

"We're different from each other aren't we?" I say as I push his white hair behind the delicately frilled ear. I trace my hand down the ink blot like patterns of his softly gradient skin.

"I think that's a fairly obvious observation, little one."

"And it's awfully strange that we can't seem to remember who we are, isn't it?"

This whole situation should make me more fearful than I am, but I'm able to keep the fear at bay as long as his skin is touching mine.

"Are you scared?" he asks softly.

"I, I don't know. I feel like I should be."

"Do I scare you?"

"No," I say truthfully.

I lean in, attempting to breathe his scent in once more, our lips getting ever so close. My body betrays me suddenly as my stomach contracts and gurgles in hunger.

"Not scared, but hungry." He smiles, lifting me from his lap, and places me gently on the bed before patting the top of my head. He walks back over to the silver button and presses it. As he holds it down, a slot opens near the floor, and two hot aluminum trays of food slide out onto the floor. He walks back over and places a tray in my hands.

The colorful assortment of spongy material steams and glistens. While the gray man looks at his tray and practically drools, I feel as though this food is strange. I poke at it with my finger, and it slides unnaturally.

"What is this?" I ask.

"Sq'aurks, of course."

He slides a two pronged utensil out of the side of the tray. He stabs into one of the blue puffs, and it wriggles intensely before he pops it into his mouth and swallows it in one gulp. My mouth drops open, and the bile rises in my throat.

"I can't eat those, they're alive!"

He looks at me strangely. "They're no good when they're dead."

"I don't think this is my people's food," I say politely, not wanting to insult his culture—not after he's been so protective of me.

"Oh, what do your kind eat?"

"Um…" I search my head. Things still feel foggy and out of place, but slowly a word materializes in my mind. I'm proud I can recall anything. "Pie, we eat pie."

"What's pie?"

"It's food, it's sweet, covered in a pie crust. You bake it," I say, my mouth watering at the thought of a peach pie, but my stomach roils as soon as I look down at the trays again. I turn away and bring a hand to my mouth.

"I don't think we have pie," he says regretfully. "I also think if you're not going to eat your sq'aurks maybe I should? To make sure my stamina and strength stay up… in case, you know, something bad happens when the doors open. I'd like to be able to protect you."

I try to push the disgust down to smile; I think the best I can give him is a half smirk. "Promise you'll at least eat them quickly?"

Without warning, he tips his tray back, sliding about fifteen of the pastel colored creatures into his mouth, swallowing, and then repeating the same with my tray.

"It's a shame you don't like these. I think they might be my favorite." He pats his stomach. "But I am sorry we don't have food more suited to your palette. Will you be alright for a few hours?"

"I mean sure, just promise me we'll find some pie if we survive?"

"I'll do anything you desire *when* we survive." His voice softens, and he inhales as he leans close to me. "Can I touch you?"

I hesitate only slightly. "Do you think maybe this room is like a one-way mirror? How can we be sure we aren't being watched?"

His face lights up. "How lucky should they be to get to see something as beautiful as you." His hand hovers over my thigh, and he makes his request again, more intently. "I'll ask again, can I touch you?"

The betrayer between my thighs screams yes, even as my brain says to wait, but sometimes your crotch yells louder than your mind.

"Yes."

He lifts me from my seat next to him, nudging open my knee so that I'm able to straddle him once more. The man pulls the oversized green dress off my shoulders, its deep vee allowing it to fall and pool at my waist quickly. His eyes focus in on my large breasts, the nipples already hardening in anticipation.

"If anyone is watching us," he whispers, "let them enjoy the view, because I will rip the head from their body for witnessing this goddess without her permission." His brow sinks down as he sucks my nipple into his mouth while his hand palms its twin.

"There's no way we're strangers," I moan, arching into his eager mouth. He looks up at me with hooded lids.

"I lied, you taste better than sq'aurks. I think I have a new favorite flavor."

His hand slides from my breast toward my throbbing sex. I hold my breath as he grabs the dress and pulls it apart at its center seam, ripping it cleanly from my body. He takes his large fingers and rubs them against my slit. They slide through wetness easily, and he tests my entrance as if unsure of its location. His eyebrows knit, and his eyes seem far off as he feels me, trailing his fingers all around my most sensitive flesh.

"First time?" I joke, even as my breathing gets ragged and I roll my hips against his hand.

"I doubt it," he shrugs, "but maybe the first time with your kind? Tell me if I do anything that doesn't feel good." His fingers find my clit.

"Shit!" I say and he pulls his hand back rapidly.

"F'tee, did I hurt you?" His face is crestfallen.

"No, good, very good," I say as I pull his hand back where my body is begging to be touched.

"We like *very good.*"

He trails his fingers back up to the sensitive nub at the apex of my thighs. He takes two of his fingers and strokes on either side of my clit. The pressure he applies tugs at the nerves, and I pant as he works my pussy. I throw my head back and rest my chin on his chest.

"That feels so good," I sigh.

I protest as he pulls his hand from me, but I stop my mewling as he puts his other hand on my exposed neck and feeds the fingers that were between my legs slowly into my mouth. Torturously, he pushes past my lips, and I taste my tangy sap.

"Do you taste how wet you are for me?" he growls, tightening his grip on my throat.

"Fuck," I groan as he takes his fingers from my mouth, grasps my cheeks between his hands, and pushes his full lips into mine. A kiss so hungry that I swear my lips are bruised. He pulls back, hoists me up by the ass, and spins us around. He lays me on the bed and places my knees over his shoulders.

I feel his breath on my pussy as he says, "I'm going to taste that pretty little cunt of yours."

He pushes his mouth against me, his tongue lapping long, hard strokes from the bottom to the top. It pushes my clit in the most delicious way. I weave my fingers through his white hair, wrapping them in the strands as if I need something to ground myself. His tongue works my clit again, and I clench my ass and lift my hips. The pleasure builds as my body tightens—I feel myself approaching a point of no return.

He lifts his eyes to me, everything below his nose obscured by my sex. His mouth makes the most obscene noises as he eats me like a peach. He tilts his head up, and my juices run down his chin, glistening in the streams of artificial sunlight.

"I like this pearl of yours very much." He opens his mouth as he begins to speak again, but I use my hand to shove him back toward the promised land.

"Now is not the time to talk," I say as he works a finger deep into my channel.

My muscles clasp around him desperately, begging for more. When he adds the second finger and curls them up to a spot I didn't know existed, I unravel. His tongue applies firm pressure as my pussy spasms. I drift toward heaven as he draws out every wave of pleasure that crashes over me.

"Jesus fucking Christ!" I scream, as I become too sensitive to touch. I push his head away and snap my legs shut, unable to handle anymore.

"I don't think that's my name," he says, chuffed, "but I suppose you can call me whatever you like as long as you let me keep tasting that delicious cunt of yours."

His face is still wet with me when he pulls up to kiss my forehead. He scoops me up to lie beside him on the bed. I can barely catch my breath as he pulls me to his side, pulling the sheet up over us.

"What about you?" I ask him.

"You say that as if tasting your nectar wasn't enough for me?"

"Is it?" I feel like he should expect more from me.

"I would do it every day should you let me," he says seriously, "but if you insist, when we get out of here I'll allow you to pleasure me." The man puffs out his chest.

"How kind of you, you strange gray man, to *allow* me to do such things." I slap at his chest as he feigns a wince.

"You sleep, little one. I'll stay up and make sure we aren't surprised—won't be long until that door opens and our fates are decided."

I want to stay up with him, but I am spent and boneless. I settle into the crook of his arm, and sleep comes quickly.

The loud clanking causes my eyes to shoot open. I'm no longer wrapped around my handsome gray stranger. Instead, I see him standing in front of the bed, holding a broken-off piece of its frame over his shoulder like a baseball bat. I pull the sheets over my still nude body as I watch the screens of the forest fade, turn to some kind of metallic structure and snap back to reveal walls with beautiful wood carvings and decor. From a forest to a stately bedroom in less than thirty seconds.

When the door swings open, a gray man in a dark suit stands there, holding two inhalers. He looks toward my gray stranger, ready to strike with brute force, then back to me in the bed. This new man rolls his eyes and scoffs.

"F'tee Ke'ain! I leave you alone for all of ten minutes and you infect yourself with harken gas, leave me to deal with those Deenz assholes, and still somehow manage to get your dick wet —even without memories?" He looks at the broken spindle from our bed. "At least let me give the antidote before you crush my skull in?"

My gray protector drops the makeshift bat to his side and reaches for the inhaler, putting it into his mouth and pressing the button. A purple mist curls from his nose as he shakes his head. He turns toward me, smiles, and grabs the second inhaler from the new man's hand. He walks to the bed and holds the inhaler up to my lips.

"Take a deep breath," he says as he pushes something into my mouth for the second time today. "Opal."

He presses the button, and I realize he has said *my* name. His eyes darken and his pupils dilate as soon as it leaves his lips.

"Gra'eth, we need to secure a pie for Opal," Ke'ain says without breaking eye contact with me. I can hear the royal attorney swear and mutter as he stomps down the hall.

CHAPTER 5
☆ROYAL DUTIES☆

☆KE'AIN

I FOLLOW Gra'eth out of my bedroom and toward the smashed clean room. I look down at the mangled bodies of two Deenz. The one at my feet stares at me with lifeless, rounded eyes. Its black blood bleeds out from the gunshot wound in its head and onto its scaled purple skin. They've been dead about as long as I've been in the panic room with Opal. I kicked the lifeless body hard in the head, my foot connecting with a thud, and more of its thick blood splatters onto the leg of my quickly thrown on suit pants.

"How in the f'tee did these scum infiltrate the palace walls, and what did they want with Opal?"

"Well, in short, I have no f'teeing clue why or how—but I do know that they're dead."

He turns to me again, his eyes giving my Opal the once over. Her small pink form is wrapped in a sheet from my bed and she's clinging to me. Her oddly fingered hands grip my hips tightly, and I can still smell her fear.

"I also know that you seemed to handle your alone time with our guest—"

I cut off what is sure to be a comment that will make me hurt Gra'eth. "What I do with Opal is very much none of you f'teeing business."

I drape my arm over her shoulder and pull her closer into the crook of my chest, a space she fits into so perfectly. She's still scared, but she juts out her chin in defiance of my friend and confidant.

"Regardless, your royal duties continue." He pulls his data pad from his breast pocket. "I'm supposed to have you on a si'bok in less than thirty minutes for the opening of tourist season." He tilts his head toward my little human. "What do you want me to do with Opal while you're working?"

Her name out of his mouth builds a growl deep in my chest that I suppress. He's trying to be helpful, but I scoff. "We aren't doing anything with Opal, she's coming with me."

I know better than to attempt to neglect my royal duties, but I'll let her leave my side over my dead body. My heart drops as I think about what would have happened if the gas had done its work before we got to the panic room. If they had taken her from me...

"Ke'ain," I hear her soft voice as she tilts her head up to meet my gaze, "don't leave me alone." Her warm breath fans over my side.

Gra'eth sighs. "I guess I'm going to need to find her something more appropriate to wear." He raises his brows. "Should I tell your parents to expect a guest?"

"I'll deal with my parents," I say, actually unsure how to approach the situation of my human guest with the king and queen.

Gra'eth brings his attention back to the data pad and types a few things. The blue light of the analyzer is pointed at Opal. She flinches as the blue laser scans over her form.

I stroke her head. "He's just getting some measurements, that's all."

She nods and lets Gra'eth continue with the scan, trusting me.

"Any favorite colors?" he jokes.

Opal opens her mouth to respond, but I answer for her. "Green."

Gra'eth narrows his eyes. "Green? You sure about that Ke'ain?"

"Do I need to make that an order?"

"Got it, green." He types into his data pad. "If we're going green, I could talk to the queen at the very least…"

"I'll handle it, just make sure the gown is perfect, Gra'eth," I bark.

"Sure, great, no pressure."

He gets away with the attitude because we're friends, but my patience wears thin. He's frantically typing into his data pad as he leaves my royal apartments. I give the Deenz one more kick before signaling to the guards to remove them. I keep Opal close to me until the guards and attendants clear the room. Wrapping both my arms around her small form and pull our bodies to face each other.

"I guess green's alright, but for future reference, I can speak for myself."

I stifle my laugh at her defiance but nod all the same. "Any color would suit you, my Opal."

She shifts nervously at the compliment but smiles.

"Thank you for staying with me. I-I don't want those assholes to take me again." Her jaw sets and anger simmers behind her brown eyes.

"Take you again?" The confusion spreads across my face. "But you applied to come here. The process is supposed to be grueling."

She blanches. "You think I wanted to be…" her face turns from white to red, shifting quickly like a cor'sopol's camouflage, "abducted?"

"I didn't know," I say. "I didn't know you were taken. I'm so sorry Opal."

I pull her into a tight hug. The Deenz hurt *my* human. I will make it my mission to murder every single one of those hive-minded bastards.

"Can't...breathe..." Opal wheezes as I release her.

"I'm sorry," I whisper. "They've got us fooled. They make it seem like human women are begging to come, to tour the galaxy."

Opal cackles sardonically. "That I wanted to leave my home? I've got news for you, big boy." She pokes her stern little finger into my chest. "Humans don't know any of this even exists!" Opal gestures broadly to me.

"How can I fix it?" I cup her head in my hands, and I pull in her scent. It is better than any ambrosia.

"Can you take me home?" she pleads, her high cheekbones wet with tears.

"Your home is off limits," I tell her gently as I can. "I have no idea how the Deenz got past the border police around your planet. It's tightly controlled."

"Oh." Her face is crestfallen.

"Even though it would destroy me to let you go, I promise if I could take you home, I would." She gives me a half smile. "I'm sure your family misses you."

"I don't really have a family anymore." Opal's face drops. "My parents died a few years back."

"I keep digging this hole deeper, Opal. I don't like to see you hurt."

"Hurting is what I'm best at though, darlin'." She laughs, but I still see the pain she tries to hide.

"Not anymore," I say. "If I can't take you home, you can make your home here."

"You don't owe me anything, you know. If anything, I owe you for getting me out of that nightmare bubble dancing." She pushes her hands lower down my abs, toward my quickly stiffening cock. "I won't play dumb and pretend that I don't know why you saved me."

Opal drops the sheet from her shoulders, unveiling her breasts. I can still see the marks my mouth left on her soft flesh as she works her fingertips over the button of my pants. She fumbles slightly, like she's attempting to flip my waist fastener open.

"Just press it," I say, my breath catching as she finally frees my cock from its cloth prison.

"I can hold up my end of this bargain." She pulls at the pants, wanting them off. She rubs her hand underneath my open waistband, "I help you out and you protect me, right?"

She looks up through hooded lids, and I suddenly realize what she's implying.

"I did not bring you here to keep you as a sex slave," I say, disgusted. I use every ounce of my willpower to push her hands away, to flip my cock up toward my waistband so it doesn't betray my sincerity. "I brought you here because..."

I stutter. I do not tell her I want to keep her forever. That I will do anything I can within my power to keep her safe, and most importantly, to keep her by my side.

"I brought you here, because I thought you wanted to be with me after our first meeting."

She looks ashamed, and I hate that almost as much as her sadness.

"I never said I didn't want to be with you."

"You never said you did either." I pause for a moment. "Do you?"

"I don't know. I went from eating some sushi in my car to being poked and prodded and shoved into a bubble for alien enjoyment. It's a lot to fucking take in, Ke'ain." Opal throws her hands up in the air, frustrated. "I just need some time. Can you let me process all this shit?"

"I said it before, but just in case you didn't hear me the first time, we'll do whatever you want, Opal. I promise." This time she hugs me, her arms not reaching all the way around my body.

"Thank you, Ke'ain," she sniffs into my chest. Her hand presses against my stiff cock. "I think it's obvious that I don't dislike you, right? I just need to figure out what being here with you entails. Can you give me a bit of time to do that?"

Her human hand presses harder, giving my cock a solid stroke.

I groan, "All the time you need."

It pains me to remove her hand from me again, but I do it. As much as I would love for her to keep going, we've got to prepare for the tourist season's opening event.

"So, what's a si'bok?" she asks.

"It's like a water cruiser, but for ceremonial events. It's jeweled and uncomfortable but an expected tradition. We'll be the tail end of the parade. I'm sorry if it'll be boring for you." I squeeze her hand in mine. "But I think we both will feel better if we don't let each other out of sight. Agreed?"

"Agreed." A small true smile creeps onto her face as she squeezes my hand back. "I don't know what kind of life you think I lead back on Earth, but boating with royalty is not an everyday event."

"Can I ask you something though, before we leave?"

"Of course Ke'ain," she says.

"What's sushi?" I can feel my translator chip struggling to place the word.

"Um, it's fish, sliced up and raw over rice. It's really good," she reminisces, obviously fond of the food.

There must be no direct translation of the word sushi in the fil'en language. Instead, visual representations of what it might be are pushed into my mind. I narrow my eyes and look at her suspiciously as images of aquatic gilled creatures fill my mind, gills like mine. I say nothing, but decide to keep an eye on how hard she bites me in the future. But as I think of her rosebud lips,

I decide maybe I wouldn't miss a bite or two if it would make her happy.

"What's that face?" She asks as I ponder how many bites from my Opal I could endure.

I shrug and guide her into the dining room, away from the crime scene that my study has become.

☆OPAL

He stares at me from the opposite side of his limo-like spaceship. Ke'ain seems more serious than before. I smooth my hands over the skirt to the green gown I'm wearing. To say it was strange to put on a dress that fit better than anything I'd ever owned is an understatement. It's as if the dress was part of my skin, its fabric similar to leather, but a bit stretchy. I don't think it's something we had on Earth though—the way the fabric flexes seems unnatural. The bust is cut low and has an asymmetrical shoulder strap. It is strange but beautiful. The green matched that of Ke'ain's suit and cape combination.

"This is like a parade, right?" I pick at the seams of the gown. We float close to the ground, and throngs of aliens flank the roadside.

"Yes, it's exactly a parade, Opal." He turns his face to look out the window. The crowds include so many different types of beings, Ke'ain's kind being the exception. Although his driver and his other staff seem to be the same species, I see none in the crowd. He sighs and pulls his lips into a tight smile.

"Don't let my parents scare you," he says. "They're a bit rigid in their expectations of me."

"I mean, that's all parents?" I ask innocently. "I think my parents could have been bad parents and I still would miss them, you know."

"That was inconsiderate of me—" Ke'ain's face drops.

"Oh, that's not what I meant at all. I just mean parents can be hard—I'm not trying to be a downer."

He chuckles. "You're not a *downer*. This whole event is the downer. The expectations put on me are the downer. These people," he shakes one hand toward the crowds and sighs, "they're the downer."

"The people seem normal to me, and they seem super excited to be here."

As far as I could tell, that is. I assume the smile is universal. But that pink guy we just passed didn't have a face as I would recognize one. Maybe I was wrong.

"Those people are killing my planet. Those people are polluting our ancestral home. I wish they'd never come here." His face flashed the same anger I saw when he looked at the dead Deenz's bodies.

"Can't you make them leave?" I softened my voice. "You're the prince, aren't you?"

He slumped a bit, sending a smirk my way. "As a prince? No. The king sets the laws, and these tourists stock the king's coffers. He'll let them ruin our oceans as long as he's got more money than anyone else in the galaxy. What if it's ruined before I succeed?" His frustration is palpable.

"Can you speak with him about it?" I ask.

"Ha, you'll see when you meet them."

"Geez, can't you buy a girl dinner before you make her meet your kin?" My joke doesn't work, and he frowns.

"Is that a human courting tradition I've missed?" He seems disappointed.

"I mean yes, but I was just joking, Ke'ain," I soothe before realizing what he implied with that statement. "Wait, are you trying to court me?"

"I thought that was what we *were* doing." His face is somehow even more crestfallen than before.

I make my way over to sit with him, somewhat ungracefully as the size of my skirts hinder my movement. Eventually, I plop down heavily next to him and place my hand on his thigh.

"Do you wanna court me?" I flutter my lashes, trying to be cute.

"Yes." He stays still under my touch.

I like the power he allows me; it pushes tingles into my chest, and I pop my tits forward a little bit. "I don't know why I'm so drawn to you... especially when it would make more sense for me to be scared, to try and figure out how to get home."

"I would take you home if I could," he says as I push my finger onto his full lips, awkwardly straddling one of his legs.

"I know home is not an option for me, but I trust you." I move my hand to his neck, wrapping my fingers around his throat. "I'm just saying I don't know why I'm so drawn to you."

I breathe in his ocean spray scent. I really do trust him, watching him slam his body against the clean room wall to get me out, trying his best to protect me. He makes me feel at ease, makes me feel safe.

Maybe it has something to do with the many orgasms he gave me earlier, without reciprocation, but I want to touch him. I want to please him now.

My lips hover a hairbreadth over his, our breathing in sync. I can't blame my actions here on some shot. There's no go-go juice this time. This is all me. I push toward Ke'ain's lips with hunger, and I probe my tongue into his mouth. When his mouth parts for me, I take his bottom lip between my teeth and bite softly. Ke'ain groans and places his hands on my hips, rocking me against his thigh.

"You better be quiet. You don't want to get caught, do you?" I ask my big gray alien.

He fumbles with a button that darkens the tint of the windows. With the push of a second button, he puts up a privacy divider between us and the driver.

"I'll be quiet as long as you promise to scream my name."

"Well darlin', hate to break it to you, but I do what I want." The fabric of my gown bunches around my hips as he pulls me directly over his dick. I brace my hands on the ceiling as he lifts me up to undo his pants button. I hear the weird fastener tech whirl, and Ke'ain's hand finds my slick entrance.

He glides his fingers easily between my lips, just barely putting pressure on my clit.

"Let me help you out first. You were more than generous earlier today." I bite my lip and move his hand to my tit.

He squeezes the tip of my breast through the gown and lifts me up. The head of his cock pushes into me. He holds me easily, as if I weigh nothing in his hands. I wish I could see him fuck me, but we're barely able to keep the volume of fabric from my ball gown tucked down enough to kiss.

"I don't want to hurt you," he gasps, "you're so small."

"Just go slow Ke'ain." I purr his name into his ear, licking the frill along its outer edge. "Promise I'll be a trooper."

He lowers my hips torturously slowly down his cock. Just when I think he's filled me completely, he pushes a bit further. I really should have looked at the equipment before I overexaggerated my capabilities. Ke'ain bites his lip, holding me still, his hands practically shaking.

"Are you okay?" he asks through his clenched teeth.

"Just give me one second," I groan with my eyes closed, trying to accommodate his girth.

It burns for only a second before my muscles relax and the slight pain ebbs into little waves of pleasure. Every tiny motion sends my nerves into a flutter.

"Opal, we can stop if it's too much—but I can't keep still much longer." His grip on me tightens, his fingers digging into my soft flesh.

I take a deep breath, pushing down on his forearms. "I want you to fuck me, Ke'ain."

His blue eyes darken, and he pushes my hips down until my ass is resting on his thighs. The feeling of fullness makes me gasp. As I settle deeper onto him, I feel something strange. Something pulses directly over my clit.

"Ke'ain, do you have a third hand I don't know about?" I ask, confusion flooding my mind. I see both his hands still grip my hips. He raises me, and whatever is sucking on my clit tugs off with a pop.

It feels so fucking good.

"Just two hands, and no silly extra fingers," he says as he lowers me onto his cock again.

He fills me deeply, and I feel it again. Something tugs at the sensitive nub again. I shudder as it sucks and pulses.

"Ke'ain, what the fuck is going on down there?" I moan.

Whatever it is, I'm not mad about it. I push my hips deeper as Ke'ain slaps my ass. He grabs the flesh as it bounces and holds on tight.

"Surely your men have cocks?" He arches his pale eyebrow.

"Cocks, yes, fuck Ke'ain." He's relentless, pulling my hips back up, the same feeling of suction makes me shudder as it rolls off me on the upswing. "What is *sucking* on me right now? Can you let me know, for science…?"

I arch up again as he drives into me. The tip of his dick hits exactly the right spot inside of me as he drags my body down onto his cock again. My clit throbs as it's grabbed again.

"It's my sucker." He pulls me up once more, and the loss of his cock inside me leaves me clenching over nothing. "Does it feel good on your human cunt?"

He growls as he pushes deep into me again, finding his rhythm as his *goddamn sucker* works my oversensitive clit.

"You have no fucking idea how good this feels."

The pop and squeeze as the sucker latches on and releases my clit is almost too much. His rhythm becomes relentless, and each stroke of his huge cock presses hard against the G-spot.

"Say my name again, Opal," he commands me.

"Ke'ain," I breathe into his ear.

"Louder," he says, as he slams his cock into me, the slickness of my sex giving him no resistance now.

"Ke'ain!" I push my hands harder into the ceiling as he wraps his arm around the small of my back. He rams into me, sweat dripping at his brow. He pulls me in, licking the column of my throat. His sucker latches onto my clit one more time before I break.

"Come for me," he groans.

My body spasms and I clutch at Ke'ain's chest. He slams into me like he's some glorious machine. My thighs shake uncontrollably.

"Ke'ain," I gasp as he pushes into me again, "it's too much!"

He picks up his pace. His body tightens, his release close. The combination of his cock and his sucker pushes me past my first orgasm. I feel a tightness deep inside my core. Ke'ain pulls at my hair, exposing my neck. He drags his teeth just below my ear.

As his cock slides out, I feel a rush of wetness flood out of me.

Did I just fucking squirt? If I had any blood left in the top half of my body, I might feign some embarrassment—but I can't be bothered. I'm so blissed-out that I feel like I might lose consciousness.

Somewhere in the back of my mind, I feel the vehicle slow. I bounce, completely boneless, on Ke'ain's cock. My eyes roll back as he fucks me senseless.

"Where do you want me to come?" he asks, his breathing laborious.

"I, uh…" Can he even knock me up? "Not on the dress."

He slides me back quickly, pulling his massive cock up onto his belly. I reach for his balls, flushed blue, and tug gently as his cock jerks.

As Ke'ain's pleasure crests and he comes onto his fancy suit jacket, the door clicks open.

We both whip our heads in shock as flashes blast into the cab.

"Shut the f'teeing door, Al'frind!" The butler stares slack-jawed before slamming the door.

Ke'ain slumps, and I swivel my legs to sit beside him once more.

"Please tell me those weren't cameras," I say.

"Do you want me to lie to you?" He swipes his hand over his face and leans over to kiss me on top of my head.

I look at the state I've left Ke'ain in. His princely suit is covered in his own release. My eyes drift down and I see the large wet spot on his open trousers.

"Sorry about the mess." I'm surprised to say I'm actually a little embarrassed to have squirted all over my alien boyfriend. There's a time and a place for that kind of thing. I don't think before a large public appearance is the most ideal time to explain mystery crotch stains.

"I'm more worried about the tabloid covers tomorrow," he sighs, grabbing a cloth from the minibar and wiping up as best he can. "We'll figure it out, though. Do you need a moment before we board the si'bok?"

My face flushes. "We're still going?" I ask, not realizing I'd have to face the public after being caught red-handed.

"It's unfortunately part of my royal duties. I'm only getting out of those if I stop breathing."

I take a moment to smooth the rumpled mess that is my skirt. "Well, I suppose it can't get more embarrassing, can it?"

With a laugh and a wink, he reaches for the door handle. "Are you ready, Opal?"

I nod and he exits the car. The flashes pop and flood the small entrance with light. I see nothing but a large gray hand as Ke'ain reaches in to escort me from the car.

I take a deep breath, setting my sandalled foot onto the soft sandy surface of my alien's planet. He pulls me to stand, and my eyes adjust to the glitter of the photographers' flashes.

Before us, in front of the crowds, in front of the photographers, stands a statuesque couple. They are clothed in the same green that Ke'ain and I don. The slighter of the two clutches at her necklace as she takes in the sight we make. The broader one simply ignores us both.

Turning on his heel, he mutters, "Let's get this nightmare over with," and tapping his ear, he speaks again. "See if

Jhr'asd can find some way to mitigate the damage my son has caused."

The slight one grabs her skirts and twirls to follow her partner, her face changing as she faces the public with a broad, regal smile.

"Opal, meet my parents," Ke'ain gestures at them as they walk away, "the king and queen of Sontafrul 6."

"Shit," I mutter under my breath. *So much for a good first impression.*

CHAPTER 6
☆THE ROYAL DISAPPOINTMENT☆

☆KE'AIN

I'M glad it is against some weird royal etiquette for the king and queen to look behind themselves when they walk in public. Some strange, outdated superstition the monarchy has held onto for goddess knows what reason. I clutch Opal's warm hand in mine, pulling her slightly in front of me to hide some of the more obvious dampness on my suit.

The si'bok is decked out in some of our island's famous pink and orange foliage. Brightly colored wreaths woven from the fronds of the mals'in tree hang about the deck. The tree is one of the symbols of the monarchy. I grip the railing and immediately pull it back. From the silver banister to my hand stretches a thick purple goo. Al'frind rushes with a cloth produced from his pocket and wipes my palm.

"Apologies, Prince Ke'ain." He's flustered as his hanky sticks to my hand. "The conditions of this ship are unacceptable; nothing like this will happen again, Your Royal Highness."

"Al'frind." I pluck the white fabric square from my palm, wrapping the remaining mess neatly in its folds as he fusses more. "I honestly couldn't care less; it's fine." All the royal domestics fall under Al'frind's authority, and I know he takes his duties seriously.

Opal shifts her eyes nervously. She must think her actions are subtle, but just as I smell her fear, I feel her bring her body closer to mine. Opal pops her small golden head underneath my raised arm.

"Anything wrong?" Her face is concerned but curious. I can only imagine how my world must seem so foreign to her.

"Not a single thing is wrong, just some weird muck on the railing." I smile and take the crook of her elbow into mine, leading her up the clean white steps of the ship.

"Some weird alien bird shit?" she asks, her shoulders relaxing as she leans into me.

"Your words are ever so eloquent, Opal," I chuckle. "It doesn't matter; let's just get this done so we can figure out what we're going to do about the Deenz and your human friends."

"You are the best, slightly overbearing alien boyfriend a recently abducted girl could have." She raises an eyebrow and smirks as I frown in her direction. "I didn't say I didn't like it, you big dummy."

"I'll take overbearing as long as you keep calling me your boyfriend."

Opal squeezes my hand, and my heart jumps. Her skin feels so different from mine. It's as if every part of her is covered in very fine fur. My skin is smooth and slick. I find myself wondering if she likes the way it feels. I love her softness, even if it's not how I thought my mate might feel.

Mate.

Every fi'len has one mate. Our scientists have spent years trying to understand the base, primal instinct. No one has cracked the code on how or why it works, but it is a truth every person in my species understands.

I always assumed I'd be one of the unlucky ones whose mate lived on the other side of the galaxy. That I'd have to find someone to settle with. That my birthright would doom me to a marriage of political alignment. My father, the greedy bastard, would auction me off to the princess with the highest bid. He wouldn't care if it was a sentient space blob as long as it coughed up the cash.

You are nothing more than a pawn. My father's words echo in my mind. We're all players in his great game of wealth. It makes me sick.

In a way, I was right when I convinced myself that my mate lay in a solar system far from my own. After all, Earth is 23,000 parsecs from Sontafrul 6. If that isn't the other side of the galaxy, I'm not sure what is.

"I'm just a little jumpy, you know, with the whole alien abduction, attempted murder, getting caught by the paparazzi banging your brains out in the car just now—" She steps forward but pulls my hand more tightly against her. I can feel the slight crackle of static electricity between our clasped fingers as we swing and brush the fabric of her gown. "But you'll protect me, right?"

"You should never doubt that, my little Opal."

As we crest the steps, the si'bok opens to a wide open-air platform, and the golden chairs are arranged in a line—*three* golden chairs. The staff knew Opal would be here, and my parents were informed of a guest. *I won't abide this snub.* Opal must catch my bristling, and I can feel the realization hit her as she surveys the scene.

"Should I just stay here?" she asks quietly, as if I would ever dare to leave her on the steps alone.

"Absolutely not," I say. "Al'frind, arrange for another chair."

Al'frind damn near flinches at my request. He drops his eyes down and hands to his sides.

"Did you hear me?" I growl.

Without raising his eyes, he mumbles, "I've been ordered to inform you that there will be three chairs, no more, no less. I was told to remove the fourth chair after your arrival, after the cruiser."

My vision blurs at the peripherals, my rage boiling. For the first time in this parade, my parents face me as they sit in the stately chairs. My father looks down his nose at me, smug and haughty. My mother doesn't look at me at all. She's ever obedient to the king.

"It's fine, Ke'ain." Opal attempts to release my hand.

I look into her eyes, and the large brown orbs glisten with insecurity over our current situation.

No.

Nope.

Absolutely not.

They will not make Opal feel less than.

I kiss her cheek and pull her into my arms. Even though her large gown is unwieldy, I carry her like one would a sleeping child. She lets out an adorable squeak as I lift her from the ground, her feet dangling aimlessly.

She bats at my chest. "Ke'ain, a warning would be nice for future reference."

I narrow my eyes and squeeze my arms around her. "For future reference, I plan to sweep you off your feet often."

Her already pink cheeks flush red as she tried to guess our next move. "Are we going somewhere else?"

"I'm happy to be the royal disappointment if that's how my father wants to play this game." I walk toward the king and queen with the precious Opal in my arms.

"Ke'ain…" My father's voice is full of warning, and he draws out my name in an almost hushed tone.

"Father," I say as neutrally as I can. I sit beside my mother and pull Opal up to straddle my thigh. "Mother, this is Opal."

Opal bites her lip nervously and nods to my parents. "Um, hi, I mean hello…"

I love the feeling of her body against me. Her weight is that of perfect comfort as she rests on me.

She finally says, "It's an honor to meet you both, Your Highnesses, or Your Majesties…" before flustering and turning away again.

I look at my father as he shifts uncomfortably in his chair.

The si'bok moves quickly through the port and into the open bay. I'm dreading the next hour so close to my father; we rarely let our paths cross. I'll do my best to enjoy Opal's ass bouncing against me as we move through the currents. I'll ignore the flash-bulbs of the photographers' cameras. I know the money shot is one that has already been taken. I'll keep it cordial with my father as long as the king can keep his mouth shut. I can only tolerate so much mistreatment of Opal before I snap.

I swear it's like he's reading my mind as I watch his jaw work.

"If you were going to dress your whore in our house's royal colors, you could have at least kept your fornicating private. Is that too much to ask of my only heir?"

His fist clenches onto the arm of his chair as his other hand waves to the crowds in broad sweeps. Every word he speaks is through a taut smile.

There's nothing but buzzing in my ears after that, and my muscles tighten. It takes me a moment to understand neither of these things are the result of my rage incarnate, but some outside force.

I clutch onto Opal as I realize we're being ejected from the deck. Heat flashes against my back as the flames from the blast push us farther into the air. The explosion's light forces my eyes shut. I can only pray we land in the water.

Opal's nails dig into my forearms. A scream builds low in her throat but quickly reaches octaves I didn't think her human body was capable of.

"WHAT THE FUUUUU—" Opal screeches just as we hit the waters of the bay like a brick wall.

☆OPAL

What in the ever-loving fuck is going on? Hot air pushes our bodies through the sky. What atrocity must I have committed in a past life to warrant the constant attacks on my safety these past few days? I feel myself slipping through Ke'ain's bulky arms and scramble to grab whatever part of him I can claw onto.

I panic as our trajectory goes from up and forward to plummeting down like bricks kicked off a rooftop.

Please let there be water. Please don't let me go splat like a June bug on a hot summer windshield.

As we slam into the waters, my skin stings. It's as though a hundred angry wasps have stung me. I want to take back my earlier plea. Maybe going splat would feel better than the burning that consumes the entire front of my body. The skin of my chest is raw and sensitive.

Worse yet, my lungs burn. We've gone straight from the smoke into the salty waters, yet I can breathe neither. I kick my legs as Ke'ain holds onto me. His powerful thighs pump strong kicks, his body is so well suited to the water.

My eyelids pinch into slits as I attempt to open them underwater. Blurs of orange and blue fill my field of vision, but I can just make out Ke'ain's face as he brings his lips to mine. He parts my lips with his tongue and fills my chest with clean air.

"Hold your breath, Opal." His voice, although distorted underwater, is clear. It's the voice of my protector.

The salt water stings my eyes, and I shut them. As he works his powerful body through the currents by feel alone, I know this is what his kind was designed to do. He cuts through the bay with movements like a dancer; we spin with corkscrew-like movements as he picks up speed. His mouth finds mine again, and he breathes sweet oxygen into me once more.

"We're almost to the surface. I've had to find somewhere to break through outside of the fire," he says.

I believe him; I can feel the heat as the fire burns on the surface of the water.

The gulp of air I take as we break the surface is all smoke and acrid tastes. I cough and splutter as Ke'ain wraps my legs around his hips. He treads water so effortlessly, keeping us afloat as he turns my head in his hands, checking me for wounds.

"Are you hurt?" he asks frantically, searching my face. "Tell me if you are in any pain."

"I think I'm alright..." I say, my gaze drifting over his shoulder to the destruction behind us.

The si'bok is unrecognizable. Smoldering bergs of debris float haphazardly throughout the bay. People scream and sirens blare. My hearing, which I didn't realize was dulled, comes back with a painful whoosh. The terrible sounds of the scene become all the louder. I cover my ears protectively just as I feel the whipping of winds building up behind us.

Ke'ain's eyes widen, and I turn my head to see a large black craft hovering over us. A hatch flips open, and a bright blue light floods around our bodies. We are lifted from the water as if every cell inside of me is being pulled toward some unseen force. I have no control over my faculties as Ke'ain and I drift apart. I can't speak, I can't scream. Some unseen force holds us, and we ascend into the metallic black craft. All Ke'ain and I can do is stare into each other's eyes right as blackness overtakes me right before we reach our destination.

CHAPTER 7
☆SAINT BEYONCE☆

☆OPAL

I OPEN MY EYES, but there's nothing. Am I blindfolded? I try to reach my hands up to clear whatever blocks my vision and realize my limbs are bound. The rough texture on my back leads me to believe that maybe I am tied to a tree.

Something that feels like wire bites into my wrists. I don't smell the smoke from the accident, but I do still smell the sea. I wiggle my toes in the sand and wonder where my shoes went, although I wouldn't be surprised if I had lost my ornate green heels when Ke'ain and I were blasted into the fucking air. Oh god, is he here with me?

"Ke'ain," I whisper, "are you okay?"

I think I hear his voice, but it's muffled. The sound of snickering fills my ears, and it's not Ke'ain's voice. My heart pounds —we're not alone.

"Well, well, well," a gravelly voice croons, "I don't see what the fuss is all about. She was easy enough to snag, wasn't she, boys?"

I hear mumbling, at least two other voices, and a slow and measured one speaks.

"Yeah boss, total cinch!"

"A total cinch?" This voice is different. "A total cinch wouldn't involve an exploding royal convoy. It wouldn't involve having to entangle the royal heir, to actively kidnap a member of the royal family. We are *not* getting paid enough for all this bullshit!"

"Don't worry Saniri, it'll all work out," the slow and measured voice says.

"No f'teeing names!" the gravelly voice barks.

"Sorry, Captain."

Heavy boots step toward me, their soles plodding through the sand. I feel a rough hand work its way up to my blindfold, fingers deftly untying it from my head. As the fabric drops and my eyes adjust, I take in the alien before me.

Parts of him seem like my Ke'ain. His build, his hands, and the small bit of his skin I can see look like they belong to the fi'len. From the bridge of his nose down is covered in a skintight suit. Its black fabric is covered in snaking lines of glowing red liquid, almost like his circulatory system is on the outside of his body. I mean, like if his blood was made of glow stick goo. The shock of black hair atop his head is in sharp contrast to Ke'ain's lighter locks as well.

His eyes burn the same bright red as the glowing tubes that pulse and twist around his form. His face is too close to mine, and his hot breath grazes the skin of my cheek. I want to push him away, I want to yell, but his entire presence is so domineering that I just keep still. I know this man will hurt me.

"So, tell me human, why's the bounty on your head so high?" He steps back slightly, crossing his arms. He doesn't look impressed by me in the least.

"I didn't even know there was a bounty..." I take a guess at his name. "Captain."

He scoffs, but continues to give me the once over. I look at his companions. They both wear dark gray coveralls, but that's where the similarities stop. One is tall and broad, his skin is dry scales of orange and red. It breaks near the crown of his head as though he is mid-shedding. His face still seems very human to me, save for the horns that decorate his jaw line. He looks incredibly annoyed. I can only guess that he's Saniri.

The other alien reminds me almost of an orc. He has rows of horns that lead to his thick black hair ornamented with golden beads and rings. He is as wide as he is tall and obviously the muscle of the crew. I'm guessing the muscles supersede the common sense on that one. Smart or not, I wouldn't want to meet him in a dark alley.

I wouldn't want to meet any of these aliens anywhere. But fuck my luck, here I am tied to a tree having to confront all of them. The small island we're on is just barely enough to house the two trees and the strangers' black craft. I scan the horizon and see nothing but more tiny clusters of sandy islands. We must be very far from the scene of the crashed si'bok.

I hear the muffled yells again and realize Ke'ain is tied to another tree behind the burly crew of space pirates. He pulls against his restraints. His suit jacket is ripped open, and the gray muscles of his chest ripple. The amount of force he's putting on his own body makes me fear that he'll rip an arm from his socket. He's blindfolded and gagged, but his head thrashes.

"Ke'ain, babe, calm down," I say unconcernedly. "I'm okay, I'm not hurt—you won't hurt me, right Captain?"

I wish I knew our captor's real name. I know, from an extensive binge watch of all of the *Forensic Files*, that captors don't like it when their victims use their names. It's humanizing. I wonder if it's the same for aliens. Or is it my name they need to hear?

"I'm Opal, by the way," I tack on for good measure.

"Well, Opal, the bounty is dead or alive." He arches an eyebrow. "Got a good reason I should waste the extra resources on my ship keeping you alive? I don't think the Deenz plan on keeping you breathing after delivery, human."

Ke'ain struggles again, the threat on my life not going unnoticed.

"Ugh, the fucking Deenz?" I screech, untethered by the mention of the hive-minded bastards.

Captain frowns and knits his brows at my outburst. "Yes, the Deenz. You are one of the best bounty contracts I've seen in a while. What'd you do to piss them off?"

My cheeks flushed with anger. "What did I do to piss off those little purple bastards? Fuck if I know! They're the ones who stole me from Earth. Why would they even want me back? They sold me like livestock to Ke'ain."

"They stole you?" Saniri asks, his gaze intense. All three aliens wait for my response.

"Yes, Saniri, they snatched my big ass right out of my car after work. I woke up here and was expected to dance in a fucking bubble. Just call me Opal the bubble babe."

He frowns. "Fer'oon, we agreed no slaves."

"No real names, for f'tee's sake." Captain—Fer'oon—runs a palm over his masked face in frustration. "I know we said no slaves, but this is just a bounty. We're not slavers."

"I don't give a shit, I'm out if she's a slave." Saniri is stern in his response. Captain Fer'oon's shoulders slump a bit and he turns to the orange alien.

"We need the money," Fer'oon says.

"I don't want that money, and you shouldn't either, Fer'oon." Saniri's response seems final.

"Don't f'teeing touch her!" Ke'ain snarls, having worked the gag from his mouth.

"Regardless of what we decide to do about the bounty, we won't touch a hair on your head, little prince." Captain Fer'oon motions for the muscled green goon to replace the gag. "Wouldn't want the royal family on our tails now, would we?"

"You blew up the si'bok! I think you're in for a world of hurt from the royal family, you idiot marauders," Ke'ain screams.

Captain swivels and marches toward the blindfolded Ke'ain. "For the record, prince, we didn't blow your si'bok sky high. We just seized the opportunity to snatch the human—we've been tracking her since the contract went out. The fact that you refused to let her be pulled into the tractor beam alone is on you." Captain Fer'oon pats Ke'ain on top of his head condescendingly. "Second thing, we're not idiot marauders, we're damn good marauders. We plan on delivering your royal ass right back to the palace. A little whiff of harken gas to inspire some fake head trauma confusion, and we might even get a hefty reward for bringing the heir home."

I curse myself for thinking that they've got a pretty good plan. Harken gas, the same thing that robbed us of our memories in the panic room, would be the perfect cover. Without the antidote, Ke'ain wouldn't remember who he was...or me. They could make a clean getaway. We're fucked.

"If you hurt her, you hurt the royal house all the same," Ke'ain says seriously.

"Why's that? Is she the palace's favorite whore?" Captain Fer'oon jokes.

"Because...because we're married," Ke'ain sputters. "You've got the Princess of Sontafrul 6 tied to a tree."

Did I hit my head harder than I thought? I stare at Ke'ain's mouth. His lip twitches nervously, his arms flexing against the restraints. I can tell he's nervous. This is a ploy to get us out safely. My alien boyfriend is trying his best.

"But if you were married, wouldn't we know about it?" the green goon asks. You can almost see the single brain cell he possesses bouncing behind his eyes.

Ke'ain opens his mouth, but closes it quickly. Shit. Ke'ain might be many wonderful things, but it appears he's not a great liar. I, on the other hand, am a great liar.

"Human tradition," I say simply. Maybe it's my years of working food service, but I can spin a tale to keep guests happy. "It's human tradition to elope, and to keep it private for everyone but close family for a month until the public ceremony."

"Why the f'tee would you do that?" Captain Fer'oon asks incredulously.

"It's a longstanding human tradition of..." Did I say I was a good liar because shit, now I'm blanking. "...of *Saint Beyonce*. It's just something that's always been done. My sweet darling Ke'ain agreed to abide by my silly human traditions after rescuing me from the slavers." I lay the sugar on thick, treating these pirates like disgruntled restaurant guests with food late from the kitchen. *Let little ole Opal make it all better for ya.*

"This little pink thing is the future queen of Sontafrul 6?" Captain Fer'oon asks with a bemused grimace.

"Fer'oon...That's a fi'len name. She is your future queen too, you bastard," Ke'ain snaps.

His comment triggers something in Captain Fer'oon—the glowing red tubes whir and his muscles twitch intensely. He points a finger at Ke'ain, and the glow in his eyes intensifies.

"I haven't been *just a fi'len* in some time, prince."

"Fer'oon, if you let us go, we'll keep quiet. We'll say we drifted off from the blast. If you just let us go, Ke'ain and I will owe you a debt," I plead. The tears welling in my eyes aren't for show.

"A debt..." Fer'oon drawls, "won't keep me flush in fuel. It won't keep our bellies full. A debt won't bribe customs officials when I try to smuggle cargo through borders. I need money."

"I'll double what the Deenz are paying you, you scum!" Ke'ain shouts.

"You could have led with that." Fer'oon laughs. For the first time, I also see Saniri smile, his wide mouth revealing long fangs where a human's canines might be. His overall vibe is far too snake-like for my liking.

"You might regret that when you see the amount." The snake alien walks toward me, and I flinch as he holds his palm up. The nails on his hand lengthen into sharp claws. He reaches behind me and, with one slash, cuts through the restraints as if they were butter. I drop to my knees at the sudden loss of support, sand kicking up into my face as I land.

Captain Fer'oon takes a small data pad out of his suit. He taps a string of numbers before tossing it to me, along with what looks like a lighter.

"You have twenty-four hours to send that amount to the account listed on the data pad. If you don't, we'll come back for you—queen or not. Wait until you can't see our ship and cut down the prince. Any sooner and we'll bomb the shit out of this little island until you two are nothing but stardust." Fer'oon lifts my chin so that I'm looking him in the eyes. "Got it, human?"

I don't know what comes over me, but I spit in his fucking red eye. He wipes the loogie from his brow. I can't help but think that my grandma would be rolling in her grave if she knew how well I could spit.

"Twenty-four hours." He flings the remnants of saliva from his fingers onto me.

I watch as the captain and his men head back into their spaceship. Fer'oon, Saniri, and the big green oaf look smug as shit as they saunter away. I hate them.

"Cut me down now. I'll rip them to shreds." Ke'ain, still blindfolded, sounds absolutely feral.

"Deep breaths, bud. I'd prefer not to be bombed into oblivion."

I watch as their cliché little flying saucer revs up and blips to light speed or some shit before making my way over to Ke'ain. I rip the blindfold off his face; his pupils are pinpricks. I kiss his forehead.

"Be calm, babe, it's gonna be alright."

☆KE'AIN

"Calm down? You could have been hurt, you could have been *killed*, Opal!"

She's out of her mind, just standing there, peaceful as can be, and stroking my arm.

"But they didn't. They didn't and we're both all right."

She keeps her eye contact with me, and there's something about her that's absolutely certain that we'll be fine. I turn my head, checking the horizon, and see their cruiser blip into nothingness as it leaves us stranded.

"They're gone Opal; you can cut me down."

"With what?" she asks, confused.

I nod to the ground. "The laser blade, just there."

"The Bic lighter?" She picks up the weapon and nearly hits the trigger that would engage the blade—which would have shot straight through her hand.

"*Opal*, don't press that." I cringe.

"Sorry!" She holds the blade on her flat palm. "How should I hold it?"

"There's a button near the top that will activate the laser mechanism. Before you press it, make sure your hand is clear of the metal portion toward the top. Click the button again if you want to turn it off."

She does as I instruct and the blue laser arches over the top of the handle. Her eyes go wide and she smiles as she clicks the button again.

"So it's like a really dangerous lighter, got it." She winks at me.

"Think you can cut me free without hurting either one of us?"

"I'm not completely helpless, you know. I spit right in Fer'oon's eyes," she gloats. Her dress is in shreds, only hanging to her perfect body by just a few threads.

"And you're telling me to calm down? You're lucky he didn't kill us for that alone."

"Ke'ain, he wants the money. We're safe if we pay him, right?"

"Safe, well, I guess that's relative. They didn't blow up the si'bok. That means someone else did. There's a contract on your head."

She frowns. "The stuff on the railing looked an awful lot like what the Deenz secrete. Do you think they did it?"

"At this rate, I wouldn't put anything past them. Maybe it's best if we get you into hiding until we can get this sorted." Even as the words leave my mouth, I know I could never be that far from her.

She scoffs and slaps my chest again, holding her palm against my pec. "You know, with everything that's happened to me recently, I don't think I want to hide. If they wanna take me, they're going to. I'd rather spend all the time I can with you."

There's a look in her eyes that has me curious as to just *how* she wants to spend our time together. She trails a finger down my torso and stops just above my waistband.

"So, let's try and get a game plan together. How are we going to do this without splitting up and sending me away to some alien version of witness protection?"

I can't tell if she's intending to be so overtly sexual, but my cock doesn't care. It presses against the seam of my trousers and begs to be touched.

"Opal, just cut me down, and we'll figure something out," I say, trying not to sound exasperated with her.

She drags her pink finger down the crotch seam of my trousers and palms the growing bulge between my thighs.

She presses her tits into me and whispers in my ear, "What if I don't want to cut you down yet?"

Opal engages the auto fastener on my waistband and sets my cock free. It rests on her belly.

"What do you want to do, then?" I ask, more curious than annoyed.

She puts her warm hand onto my cock, but holds it still. As much as I try to arch up, to force some movement between her pretty little fingers and my engorged dick, the restraints hold.

"I want you to tell me what we're going to do. If it's a good answer, maybe you'll get a reward." Opal smiles. "Maybe I've got a fear boner, but I kind of like seeing you trussed up like this, Ke'ain. I have a feeling this might be the only way you let me pleasure you for once."

F'tee me, Opal is so devious at this moment I barely recognize her.

"If you keep your hand on my cock, I don't think my brain will get enough blood to come up with any good answers for you." I bite my lip as she tortures me by simply not moving.

When she squeezes my dick, I moan like a f'teeing virgin.

"Aw, poor Ke'ain. I think you can figure something out."

She leans in and licks my ear lobe. My cock jumps in her hand.

"We. Stay. Together," I manage to get out.

Her hand pumps me once, sliding the precum from my cock's head down its length. She adds her other hand to cup my balls, tugging them down softly. It makes my sac instantly want to pull in. When I would give her anything just to keep moving, she stills.

"Great answer, babe. Now, how are we going to do that?" She kisses me softly, but pulls aways as I seek her mouth again with my own. I love the way her fist looks clasped around my cock.

"You marry me, we declare war against the Deenz, I murder every single one of them with my own hands, and I fuck you every single chance I get for the rest of our lives," I scramble to get out.

Opal falters. "Funny. Let's be practical, though."

Funny? "I wasn't joking. As princess, you'd have the entire fleet for your protection. I'd make it so it's like the Deenz never existed. I'd wipe every trace of them from the universe."

"You don't want to marry me," she whispers, letting go of my dick and looking at her feet. "It was a good idea to have them let us go. It's okay, Ke'ain."

"What in the world are you talking about? I do, I will." I wish I could put my arms around her. F'tee these restraints.

"No one marries the thick, funny, slutty girl. Shouldn't you find some fi'len princess to rule the country? I barely know how anything here works." The confidence that oozed out of her before is gone.

"I don't want some fi'len princess. I want you, Opal. I've wanted you since the first time I saw you. I don't care about anything else. I'll teach you everything you need to know. I want to marry you, I want to rule with you, I want to have children with you."

She looks at me, tears in her eyes. "Who knows if we can even have kids together, Ke'ain!"

Opal forces out an awkward chortle.

"So, we'll adopt. I don't give a shit. I want you. *You're my mate.*"

I'm sure Opal is. A weird realization to have—tied to a tree, my cock out, and with her crying in front of me. But I've never been more sure. When I thought the marauders would hurt her, when I thought they might kill her, I knew then I would do anything to take her place. I would do anything to keep her safe.

"Are you sure?" she asks, wiping the wetness from her cheeks.

"I love you," I say. "I'll even subscribe to your weird human tradition of Saint Beyonce."

She clasps my head between her hands, pushing up to her tippy toes, and kisses me hard.

"I made that up, you dummy."

"You're a good liar. I'll need to remember that." I smile, raising my eyebrow...

"You are just the world's worst liar."

Just as I'm about to ask her to cut me down, she drops to her knees in front of me and places her hands on my hips.

"Opal, what are you doing?" I ask.

"Giving you your reward. Your answer was more than satisfactory," she says right before she pulls my cock into her mouth.

I watch her lips envelop me. *Thank you, Saint Beyonce.*

☆OPAL

His cock is too big for me to take into my mouth all at once, so I work my hands together toward its base. I won't lie and pretend that I don't give a mean sloppy toppy, but I've honestly never wanted to blow a guy as much as I do now.

Ke'ain loves me.

Part of me doesn't want to believe it, after years of lackluster human men doing whatever they can to get into my pants and then ghost me, that Ke'ain would want to stay. But I never thought I'd get abducted by aliens either, did I?

As I suck Ke'ain's cock, I eye the sucker that rocked my fucking world earlier today. For something that feels so good, it looks so unassuming. I move my mouth to the transparent cupped skin where the sucker resides and give it a lick.

"Does it feel good when I touch it?" I ask.

"I love anytime you touch me, Opal."

"So, not as good as your dick." I tap the rubbery bit of flesh. "What's it for?"

"Biologically?" he asks and I nod. "It holds the female to my body during mating; it makes more sense when you're underwater. The fi'len females have anatomy that helps with that."

"Well, can I say, regardless of its intended use on your species, I sure as fuck love it on my pussy." It's like Ke'ain's body was made to get me off.

Is it weird that I'm literally savoring the taste of his cock? I suck down his clean citrusy flavor and get worked up when my big alien moans. He pulls against the restraints and some sick part of me likes that they might hurt a little.

Honestly, who am I right now? I wish I still had my iPhone; I really want to text my therapist and ask what the hell is going on with my psyche. I do know that I will fucking marry this man... well, alien. He's more man than any other Chad, Terrin, or Jon back home. Fuck those Tinder douche nozzles.

I will marry this fucking man.

I move my hands to his hips and run my nails down his thighs. I push him further down my throat. It burns for just a second before crossing the hilt and sliding even deeper as I try to accommodate his impressive length.

"Good girl." Ke'ain's voice quivers, and he manages the tiniest of thrusts.

I gag a little bit, but I think he likes it. He drives himself into me again as much as his restraints allow him to move.

"Do you like it when I swallow your big cock?" I ask as I come up for air, but don't let him respond before I go down on his twitching member—running my tongue along the vein near the bottom.

"I won't last much longer," Ke'ain pleads. "Cut the restraints. I want to be inside you."

"And I want to swallow your cum, so get over it."

Ke'ain's eyes go wide as I pick up my pace. I use one hand to roughly work his shaft for what my mouth can't take and the other to cradle his balls. I feel them tug into his body. His cock throbs with every thrust of my head. I graze my teeth lightly over the sensitive shaft on the last thrust, and he floods my mouth with a salty burst.

I look up, and see his head thrown back, the column of his throat flexing as he grits his teeth. I swallow like it's the last water on the planet. His cock pulses as his body slumps against the restraints.

His breathing is ragged. "Opal, you're so perfect, I...I..."

The poor boy can't catch his breath.

"Don't worry, I'll let you repay the favor later," I say.

I flip open the weird, dangerous Bic lighter and carefully cut the wire holding Ke'ain to the tree. He doesn't drop as dramatically as I did, but turns around to wrap his arms around me.

"I'll never let you go, you know." He presses his face into the crook of my neck and breathes deeply.

"Good."

CHAPTER 8
 ☆QUICK & DIRTY☆

☆KE'AIN

WE'RE STILL dusty with the black sand from the island as we stand in the cargo bay of the tactical cruiser. I rub my wrists absentmindedly, the stress marks still deep blue from the tinsel wire the bastard marauders bound me with. As I rub them my mind wanders to Opal's red flushed lips wrapped around my cock, and some of the anger recedes. I instinctively wrap my arm around her back and pull her into my side. In front of us stands Duke Raf'ere of the Liin'gan Reefs. He's also my cousin, and a total f'teeing dick.

I hate his pretentious face and his ominous looking scars

"So, cousin," he says, "you're telling me your human–"

"Opal," I correct him.

"Sure, Opal." He gestures to her with his hands. "The human Opal is your mate?"

"Correct," I say.

My patience wears thin with his flabbergasted look. Although I am grateful he picked us up so quickly after Opal *mercifully* cut me down, I'm annoyed that his number is the one I know by heart and was the only one I could think to enter into the data pad left by the marauders. Our childhood friendship somehow made that small bit of information a core memory.

He crosses his arms, and the green fabric of his suit bunches over his over-inflated biceps. They're merely vanity muscles that serve no purpose other than puffing up his already incredible ego.

He raises his tiresome little eyebrows and drags in a labored breath through his nose. I bite the inside of my cheek so I don't raise a hand to deck him across his jaw.

"And you, the heir apparent to Sontafrul 6, want to marry this human, Opal, *today?*"

"Was my intent unclear?" I ask.

"Crystal clear, cousin," he says with his face full of confusion, "but are you sure you suffered no head trauma in the explosion? I could have a medic come from the bridge and just give you the once over."

"For f'tee's sake, I'm of sound mind." I turn to Opal, her dress still in tatters as she looks up at me as though I hold the moon in my hands. "Call a priestess to meet us at the reef hold. We will be wed as soon as possible."

Raf'ere runs his blocky hand through his slicked-back white hair. "There are other things that might need to be taken care of first, Ke'ain. Things that might take priority over thinking with your cock..."

"Raf'ere listen here you little—"

My anger is cut short by the cargo bay doors swinging open, and several members of the King's Guard enter in formation, putting their blasters onto their hip holsters as they take a knee before me.

"All hail King Ke'ain!" they shout in unison.

My cousin's face softens slightly. "Ke'ain, your parents are dead."

☆OPAL

Shit, shit, shit.

I am not the comforting type. When my parents died, I just kind of shut down. It's as if I couldn't remember how to be Opal.

"You're not allowing yourself the proper space to grieve," my therapist would tell me.

But if I allowed myself the space I needed to truly grieve them, I'm not sure there would have been space left for anything else. I wouldn't have been able to work, I wouldn't have been able to go about the stupid day-to-day things that simply needed to get done. I would have been stuck in a perpetual cycle of screaming, crying, and throwing up.

"Ke'ain," I whisper as I clung to his biceps, "I'm so sorry."

His arm stiffens as he scrutinizes the kneeling guards. I wonder if it feels the same as when my parents died—or if the burden of being the sole heir of a space kingdom somehow made it worse?

"We need to get you back to the palace right away," Raf'ere says tenderly. Raf'ere's is slightly different from Ke'ain in his appearance. He possesses the same grey skin, white hair, and build as my alien. Small iridescent scales are scattered along his cheekbones and jawline. They glint pink and teal depending on the reflection of the light. The scales are beautiful, despite the deep scars that blemish the skin near them.

It must pain him to be gentle. The tone at which he's speaking is not his usual cadence. We are both bad at comforting, I see.

"I stand by what I said. I want to marry Opal first." He places a hand over my own, still clasped to his arm.

"Are you sure?" I ask.

When Ke'ain looks at me, his eyes soften. "I only wish I could wed you without thrusting you into the position of queen, Opal.

There will be parts of us that always belong to our people. In a way, you must marry them as well."

I pull my shoulders back and look the alien I've come to love in the eyes. "As long as we can stay together, I'd marry every person on this damn planet."

"The human Opal is my future queen?" Raf'ere's lips twitch. It's very obvious he wants to say something that might lead to Ke'ain's fist meeting his mouth.

"Arrange a priestess to meet us at the palace. Opal will be your queen by the end of the day."

Raf'ere stares at Ke'ain for a beat, shrugs, and turns back toward the cargo bay doors. "I would recommend letting Gra'eth know ASAP. You're gonna need some damage control in this situation, whether you want it or not."

"I'll handle it. Just do your part." Ke'ain is stern in his response.

"I am sorry about your parents."

Raf'ere's mouth twists into a frown. Kindness once again proves not to be his strong suit. Ke'ain slumps as his cousin attempts his condolences.

"I am too." Ke'ain says.

"All hail the king," Raf'ere mutters before making his way through the doors.

———

I peel back the mylar wrapper of the "protein serving." It's a drab khaki color and reminded me of the SlimFast bars my meemaw pushed onto me as a preteen when the family hips came in. But to be honest, I'd rather have a shitty peanut butter and fake chocolate flavor than whatever this savory fish-flavored power bar was.

My stomach grumbles in approval of the incredibly bland sustenance that fills it. The sawdust-like texture expands as I eat it, and I feel fuller than I have in a long while with every bite that passes by my lips.

I tug the sleeve of the gray jumpsuit Raf'ere provided me with. The arms are about two feet too long. Despite rolling them up, they keep slipping past my fingertips. When I took off the dress I'd arrived in, it was entirely in shreds. At least I was covered now. I frown down at the bar as I take another bite.

At least it's not the steaming and wriggling sq'aurks, right, Opal? Ke'ain might have great qualities, but his love of the disgusting-looking puffballs was not one I found endearing.

I wonder if his tough guy act will falter later tonight once we're alone. If maybe he's still in shock. I just know that I can be there for him whatever might happen. I know numbness is better than grief sometimes.

As if summoned by my thoughts, Ke'ain peeks around the doorway to the mess hall. He frowns at the face I must be making as I work the leathery texture of the food with my teeth.

"Opal, I'm sure we could ask the cooks to find something more pleasing to your human palette," he says with a cringe.

"They shouldn't have to cater to me. If I'm staying here with you, I better start getting used to things in your culture," I say between tough bites.

"I agree, there are some things you'll have to get used to—but can't we make just a few accommodations for your comfort?"

Like a dirty old man, I wiggle my eyebrows. "You've been more than accommodating for my comfort, Ke'ain."

He takes the protein bar from my hand and tosses it into a nearby bin. Pulling another mylar packet from the mess hall shelf, he dumps its contents into a bowl. It looks powdery and dry, and I crinkle my nose.

"That's supposed to be any better?" I ask.

Ke'ain chuckles. "Awful impatient little human, I'm not quite done yet."

He moves his four fingers over to a button on the wall. As he depresses it, hot water pours from a spout and fills the bowl. The powdery substance expands and thickens, reminding me of oatmeal.

"What is it?" I ask him, puzzled.

"It's dried grin'oj root." He passes me the bowl. "A very popular breakfast among the children here."

"So you're saying I have the taste buds of a fi'len child?" I arch an eyebrow dubiously.

He pulls a small ornate bottle from his jacket pocket. "What I'm saying is that it's easy to eat, and you need sustenance, little Opal."

Ke'ain removes the lid of the bottle and sprinkles something brown over the bowl of steaming mush. The powder scents the air as it drops into the steaming porridge.

"Ke'ain, I might be hallucinating, but is that cinnamon?" I pull the familiar scent into my lungs and am instantly hit with bittersweet memories of Christmas past.

His eyes light up. "It is! Is cinnamon something you like?"

"Yeah, it's a pretty universally liked human flavor," I say, my mouth watering.

"Well, my sweet Opal, you are in luck. It is indeed *universally* liked. In fact, the fi'len who managed to get a smuggled cinnamon tree to Sontafrul 6 received a medal of honor from my great-great-grandfather." He puffs up his chest with pride.

"You're kidding right?"

"Cinnamon was one of the things that first made us the richest planet in the galaxy. With the restrictions surrounding Earth, men have died attempting to smuggle it off world."

"That's some spice road bullshit," I say, ignoring his confusion as the Earth history reference. "Couldn't you just like synthesize it or something with your fancy alien tech?"

"We tried, it's just…" He pulls his mouth to one side of his face and furrows his brows. "…just not the same."

I take the bowl and the tiny shovel-shaped spoon Ke'ain

hands me. For the fi'len having such large hands I find it funny that their eating utensils feel small in my grip.

I take a bite and am pleasantly surprised at the mild sweet flavor. It's not my favorite consistency, but the cinnamon really does make it edible. I can't parse what it reminds me of, maybe sweetened mashed potatoes? In any case, it's far more enjoyable to eat than the protein bar.

"Thanks, babe," I say as the warm porridge fills me up. "Maybe once things settle down, you'll let me experiment in the kitchen a bit. Maybe I can find something we both like?"

He leans against the door frame and his eyes rake lovingly over my body.

"I'd eat dirt if it made you happy, little human."

"I'd rather you eat me, big boy," I joke as I scrape the last bit of porridge from the bowl.

But Ke'ain, who to be fair, still has yet to understand the finer points of my human humor, grins and reaches for me.

"Not now!" I yelp playfully as he throws me over his shoulder and slaps my ass. The plastic bowl and spoon clatter to the floor dramatically.

"You would deny me after the wealth of cinnamon I just supplied you?" Ke'ain laughs.

"Wealth? Since when do a few sprinkles of spice equal wealth?" I slap at his back and try to avoid eye contact from the others in the ship's corridors.

"The bottle cost more than most of these soldiers' yearly pay, just for your information," he says, running his hand up the back of my thigh, dangerously close to pussy.

"Ke'ain, Jesus fuck, it's just cinnamon!" He pushes the data pad mounted on the wall outside his cousin's chambers, and the door whooshes open. We enter and it snaps shut behind us. Ke'ain tosses me like a sack of potatoes onto the large bed.

He runs his hands over my oversized gray jumpsuit, putting his palm over my sex and drawing his eyes up to my own.

"I'd give you all the cinnamon on this planet if it would keep you happy." Ke'ain slides his hand down and traces the crotch seam of the jumpsuit. I can feel the pressure of it on my clit, even through the layer of rough fabric.

"Even if you made me eat those awful-looking sq'aurks, I'd still be happy as long as I was here with you." I sit up and stretch my hand out to cradle his cheek.

Ke'ain places his hand over mine, and his mouth twitches into a smarmy grin. "Well, at least I'll save money on cinnamon."

"Way to miss the point there, Ke'ain," I say as he presses his lips into mine. The force of his kiss puts me flat on my back.

Ke'ain steadies himself over me with a hand on the bed. I wiggle my hips, wanting nothing more than to remove the barrier of clothing between us. Ke'ain grabs one of my hands and pins it over my head, and I arch my hips higher, my heart-beat throbbing in my ears and between my legs.

An electronic beep breaks our lustful concentration as Raf'ere's annoyed voice comes over the speaker. "Officer Hy'rul, please report to the bridge."

As if broken from a trance, I can suddenly smell my own armpit BO. *I absolutely reek!*

"Oh my god Ke'ain, why didn't you tell me I smelled this bad?"

The gray alien leans in close, despite my squirming and protesting, and takes a big whiff.

"I love it," he says as he darts his tongue out and licks the sweat out of the hollow of my pit.

"Ke'ain, first absolutely not, second just because you're into this doesn't mean I want to stink." I push his chest and roll to my side.

"I suppose if you must wash, there's a water closet just behind that door there." He points to it and palms the bulge in his pants as he looks me over seductively, making no attempt to hide his actions. "Want help washing?"

"You know it's not the first time I've bathed, right? I'll be fine."

Despite my sarcasm, I know what he's implying, but for some reason, I want to be a little bratty. Okay, more like I like being a brat *all the time*.

"As you wish, Opal," he says, putting his hands behind his head as he seems to settle in for a nap.

Seeing him on that bed, though, I get unsettlingly mushy. I'm not sure if it's despite or because of the massive erection straining the fabric of his pants—but it probably doesn't hurt.

"Thanks, for the food, for the stupid expensive cinnamon, for saving me, for you know... just all of it."

Ke'ain peeks open one eyelid. "Thank you for trusting me... and thank you for letting me keep you." His cheeky expression is replaced by a far more serious one.

Biting my lip, I look away. Ke'ain's gaze is too intense, and despite my stink, I'm still horny as fuck.

Step one, shower. Step two, get banged.

Opening the door to the bathroom, I figure I'll just have to treat him extra nicely once I smell a bit better.

The shower itself is a stainless steel box. Showerheads are all lined up at varying points in the wall, like it was made to spray as large a surface area as possible.

I look at the panel of buttons and try my best to figure out what works what. Eventually, after blasting myself with a gust of cold air and maybe activating the self-cleaning function, I figure out which button supplies the hot water.

I pull the weird little zipper at the neck of my jumpsuit, the whole thing unlatching as soon as I touch it. The jumpsuit drops to the ground, so oversized on my body, it has nothing to anchor itself on like it would on the body of the fi'len.

The first blast of hot water hits my skin and makes me shiver with pleasure. I'd always been a shower girly back on Earth.

The blast of warmth makes me long for my fruity smelling body washes and scrubs. I literally had a shower playlist for the hour-long, almost too hot, showers I would take on lazy days. I missed it all, except for the removable showerhead—Ke'ain more than made up for that.

I close the glass door and lean up against the back of the metal stall. Pushing my back up against the line of jets, I let them work on one of the many knots my hips had acquired. I wondered if we really held trauma in our hips like my yoga teacher used to preach. Even if we don't, the pressure feels amazing.

Eventually I figure out what button on the shower's panel provides soap. It doesn't smell like passion fruit, unfortunately. It does remind me of hospital soap and seems to be more antibacterial than a feast for the senses.

Somehow I'm not surprised that a world that thinks cinnamon is worth dying for doesn't have many exciting scents.

For a moment I imagine Ke'ain's face if I gave him a bite of pineapple. It would literally blow that bland little alien's poor mind.

☆KE'AIN

Opal hums in the water closet, her melodic little voice drifting through the crack in the door. The jets of warm water fog the doors to the shower unit. My cousin, per protocol, has given us his own quarters for the journey. The room is overdone, gilt in gold, and pretentious. It is Raf'ere incarnate. I don't know why I can't help hating him—he's done much for me today. He's come to our rescue, and now he's bringing us back to the capital, to my coronation.

I raise my eyes to the six-foot-tall painting of Raf'ere in his royal suit. *Nope, I still can't stand him.* He's the kind of person who commissions an oil painting of himself for his own room. His shoulders are broader and his face more handsome in the painting, but the scarring along his jaw is smoothed.

I should be kinder, more diplomatic, more reserved in my

distaste for him. Especially since my family's numbers have dwindled today. *My parents are gone.*

I wonder when the grief will hit, and if it ever will. I am sad, but somehow I am not overwhelmed. Parts of my heart, mostly for my mother, are broken. Even though her austere demeanor rarely dropped, I saw flashes of the mother she might have been. Like how she knew I hated the food served at state banquets and would secretly pass me sq'aurks under the table. She never truly felt like my mother. My wet nurse, Tro'kip, cared for me in that way—and she died years ago. I grieved Tro'kip like she had given birth to me herself. I think my mother resented me for it.

I gave up on my father long ago. There was no secret kindness between us. I was tasked with marrying well and bringing him a large dowry. He didn't care for me besides that.

I always had Al'frind, though. He had given me more fatherly advice in a single night than my father had given me in an entire lifetime. I won't pretend that the sadness of their deaths didn't sting. It was like the pricking tentacle of a poke'en, its sting quickly turning to an ache. I couldn't help feeling as though I *should* be sadder. Would I be coerced to put on a more sorrowful facade for the sake of the monarchy?

A wail from the water closet breaks me from my melancholy. Opal's slightly off pitched but enthusiastic singing fills the room.

I wonder if this is some folk song from Earth. Rising from the bed, I pad over to the slightly cracked door. I push it wide with one finger, and a blast of steam hits me.

Opal's body faces away from me, the jets sluicing water down the beautiful curves and rolls of her back. She turns her head and mimes singing into an imaginary microphone, her face warped with passion as she performs unknowingly for an audience of one. The rows of water jets hit her on the left side of her body, the nozzles in a vertical line all along the stainless steel wall.

She throws her head back, her wet hair whipping over her shoulder. "Dah dah do do dah do dah!" Her pink skin is flushed red from the warm water. I can't help myself and start a slow clap.

Opal peeks open one eye over her shoulder, spotting me, her posture going from triumphant to meek immediately.

"Oh shit, I'm sorry Ke'ain... I just haven't had a real shower since I was taken, and god have I missed them." She bites her swollen lip. "I should be taking care of you instead of hosting my own private karaoke session."

I don't ask what a karaoke session is. I'm speechless as she faces me. Her bountiful breasts are flushed pink from the warm water, her nipples stand at attention as she moves from the jets' spray.

"What can I do to help?" she asks as I watch the water bead over her body.

Only for a second do I let my mind wander and imagine what I would feel if I lost Opal today. I feel the sharp bite of grief as it gnaws at my heart almost instantly. The pain burning my chest before I shove it back down.

Opal is here, with me.

"Don't apologize on my behalf," I say as I activate the fastener on my waistband. My trousers drop at record speed.

Opal arches an eyebrow as she appraises my intent, but her countenance is caring. "It's okay to not be okay, you know."

"I'm okay as long as I'm with you."

I push the glass door to the shower unit open and Opal reaches her hand up to my face on her tiptoes.

"Together, forever."

I grab her face between my hands, pulling her in for a bruising kiss. I break the kiss and see that her eyes are wide, as if I've caught her off guard.

"Together forever, I promise."

I slip my body into the shower unit with Opal, running my hands over her slick skin. I pepper kisses down her neck, pushing her up against the steel walls. She instinctively pushes her hips back against my cock. I use my knee to nudge her legs apart, my fingers easily finding her slick pussy.

"Jesus fuck, Ke'ain," Opal breathes into my chest, and I tease the opening of her sex.

"Prepare for acceleration, proceed to jump seats, secure loose articles." A friendly but obviously computer voice floods the room. My little human pushes on my chest.

"Should we..."

I pull my finger from her cunt and drag it over her lips to shush her. She quiets, and then I push my finger into her mouth, letting her taste herself.

"You think I can't hold you down?" I ask her.

"Still mad that I kept you tied up?" Opal bites down softly on my finger.

I smile, and turn Opal to face the wall—maybe a little roughly after she brings up the bondage. The rows of jets sputter as they spray warm water down the front of her body. I push her further down, pulling her hips toward me. Opal's body seizes slightly as I adjust her.

"Shit!" she yelps.

"Are you all right?"

"Yes, um, the jet...is placed in a *very good* spot." She moans and wiggles her hips slightly.

I reach my hand toward her clit. The pulsing warm waters hit the sensitive little nub directly.

"Do you want to come on my cock?" I growl into her ear as I nip at its lobe.

"Fuck me," she moans.

I fist my cock twice and guide it into her welcoming warmth. She turns her face, her cheek pressing hard into the wall. Her skin squeaks as it shifts and drags against the metal. I take my free hand and wrap her golden hair around my fist. I pull her head back and roughly press our mouths together again. Each thrust of my hips is met with a slap of skin as I drive deeper into my flawless mate, into my forever. Her skin squeaks and her voice sighs in a relentless rhythm.

"Prepare for acceleration, countdown starting now. Ten, nine..." The voice on the broadcast system begins the countdown, and the floor shifts as the pulsar engine engages. Opal pushes her hips toward the pressurized jet of water, and her cunt constricts quickly over my cock.

"Ke'ain, I'm so close."

Her body starts to shake as I lose control. I grip her ass and pound into her, my gray hands leaving red marks on her skin.

"I want to fill you up, sweet Opal. I want to keep you full of cum every single day until we both become stardust. I want to—"

"Three, two, one." The computer's monotone voice finishes its countdown, and the thruster engages.

The force of the propulsion pushes our bodies together. Opal's hips grind against the nozzle and shudder as she finds her release. Her sweet pulsing cunt consumes my cock until I'm left gasping as she milks me for every drop I'm worth. The muscles of her sex are enough to bring me over the edge. My sac tightens and I spill into her. Unable to move, I bite her tender shoulder, stifling my moans.

The G-force keeps us pressed together, intensifying our orgasms as we're both anchored in place. The jet is still pounding Opal's clit with warm pressurized water, extending her orgasm further, and every spasm of her muscles pulls me further into bliss.

"I love you," she pants.

"Forever," I say as we stay stuck together from the impelling force of the tactical cruiser speeding back to the capitol.

I squeeze the hand still stuck onto her glorious rump. I would be fine should we be stuck like this forever. Opal feels like paradise.

"Cruiser arriving at port in ten, nine, eight, seven, six, five, four, three, two, one," the computer blares.

With a jolt, our bodies are released from the wall and our legs crumple beneath us. We land on our asses in a pool of quickly draining water, my head thudding slightly off the glass door.

Opal takes in a sharp gasp of air just as she's hit in the face with a blast of water from the jets. She pushes her hand up to block the fine spray and starts to laugh. Her laughter is so pure and melodic, I can't help myself and begin to laugh too. I pull her onto my lap, and we're both laughing so hard that tears are welling in our eyes. Opal throws her head back, and snorts through her nose—and if I thought I was losing it before, that adorable noise sets me over the edge. My chest heaves with a howl I can't control.

How bizarre that the universe has brought us together. How small was the chance we would ever meet each other? I say a silent prayer to the goddess in thanks.

Opal wipes a tear from my cheek, wraps her arms around my neck, and squeezes me tightly as she attempts to get control of her breathing.

"Come, let's dress and greet your future kingdom." I stand and pull her up.

She looks at me, slightly flustered but still chuckling. "You know, I'd really love to wash the baby gravy off myself before the grand debut. I'd prefer not to inspire the photographers with anything but my *natural beauty* after last time?" She winks and flips her hair dramatically.

I snort again as my translator chip sends ridiculous images to my brain of what it thinks baby gravy might be. The human language is an enchanting one.

CHAPTER 9

☆THE OLD WAYS☆

☆OPAL

I'M SURROUNDED by armed fi'len guards, their iridescent armor glinting as we rush down the incredibly long palace hall lined with windows. Between the twenty or so guards surrounding me, and Ke'ain clutching me to his side, I can't see anything.

"So, is there a game plan?" I whisper into Ke'ain's torso as my little human legs do double time to keep pace with the hulking aliens around me.

"Yes, we marry, I protect you, we annihilate the Deenz." Ke'ain tosses me a bright smile.

"Yeah yeah, I've got that part." I roll my eyes. "I mean right now, where are we headed?"

"I assume we're on our way to meet with the king's council. I'll need to appoint the hand of the king before we can do anything." He peers around the guards' heads, as if he just now realizes he doesn't know where we're being led either.

"I suppose that's pretty important. Who are you going to appoint as hand of the king?"

"Well, there's only one person I trust to do it..." The guards stop and swing open the double doors to a large conference-style room. The table at its center looks as though it's made of some kind of black obsidian. Along one side several stuffy-looking fi'len are seated, including a familiar face. "Gra'eth."

Gra'eth pushes back from the table, his high-backed black chair clattering to the ground as he rushes toward us.

"I thought you were both dead!" His eyes are wide and almost wet as he pulls Ke'ain into a crushing embrace. "Your parents, Ke'ain..." He pulls back hesitantly.

"I know, Gra'eth, I know."

"All hail the king," Gra'eth whispers as he bows his head.

"And your future queen," Ke'ain says as he presents me with a flourish of his hand.

Gra'eth shoots up straight as a rod and narrows his eyes before shaking his head slightly as if to clear his thoughts.

"My queen," he says, bowing as he takes my hand and kisses it.

Queen. The reality of my situation hasn't sunk in yet. I am a college dropout. How am I going to rule a whole goddamn planet? Is there a *Royalty For Dummies* handbook I can check out of a space library?

Ke'ain clears his throat. "Gra'eth, feel free to release her hand any moment." The annoyance is palpable in his voice.

"Oh let him fuss, Ke'ain," I scold.

Gra'eth releases my hand quickly, despite my complaint. He stands and smiles, as if we're the prettiest thing he's seen all day.

"My apologies, King Ke'ain," Gra'eth says, switching to a more formal speech pattern, "we have pressing business to attend to. You must name your hand. I've got a dossier of suitable candidates." He pulls his data pad from his jacket pocket.

"You are my hand," Ke'ain says plainly.

Gra'eth eyes go wide and he stutters, "Y–your Majesty, I

think if you just review the list, you'll find a more suitable candidate."

Ke'ain places his palm onto Gra'eth's chest and says, "You're who I trust the most, discussion over," before walking past the dumbfounded attorney and leading me to the pair of ornate chairs and the head of the table.

As we sit, Gra'eth straightens his sleeve, takes a deep breath, and makes his way to the chair on the other side of my betrothed.

"Now that we have that sorted, our next order of business is my marriage to Opal. Opal..." He turns to me, his face flushing blue, embarrassed. *He doesn't know my last name.*

"Opal May Legare," I whisper to him as I squeeze his hand. Surnames seem so unimportant after the misadventures we've had.

"Opal May Legare and I will be married—only then will the coronation take place."

Everyone seated at the table whispers, and the disapproval in the room is palpable. There's only one face at the table that displays anything beyond confusion or disgust, and that's Gra'eth's.

"I think that's an excellent plan, my King," Gra'eth says as he folds his arms over his chest and settles back in his chair. The other fi'len sit slack-jawed, but say nothing.

I turn to my alien. "Do your other council members take issue with our marriage?" I ask him in a hushed tone. Their faces lead me to believe this will not be an easy transition.

"If the hand sees it fit, who are we to question the king?" a weathered fi'len sitting next to Gra'eth says as he bows his head.

This is too easy. Why on Earth, I mean Sontafrul 6, is everyone suddenly cool with me? Why is Gra'eth enthusiastically on board with *the human Opal* being his queen? I eye him suspiciously as he smiles to himself. The damn stick in the mud looks like he's on cloud nine.

"Gra'eth, you're okay with me as your queen?" I ask, leaning over my future husband's broad chest with eyebrows raised.

He turns his head lazily toward me, his eyes soft. "Who am I to deny Ke'ain his mate?"

I narrow my eyes, still skeptical of the lack of his usual bitching. *God, what's wrong with me?* I know I should be fine with something finally coming easy to me...but it feels wrong.

Quit letting your life be a fucking sob story

I force a broad smile and address the council. "Thank you for allowing me this great honor. I hope to learn how I can best serve this beautiful planet."

They let their expressions soften, but I know they're still dubious about me.

"Should we find out any of Opal's human customs to include in the ceremony?" Gra'eth inquires.

Again, since when does he give a shit about my human customs?

"Saint Beyonce maybe?" Ke'ain elbows me. I fucking love that doofus.

"No, let's stick with the ceremony you would normally do. I'll need to learn your customs to rule these people. Maybe this is a good first step."

Ke'ain beams at me. "I think that's an excellent idea, Opal. Let me handle everything."

As Ke'ain rises from his seat, so do the other men surrounding me. I place my hand on his before he can leave.

"Should we, well," I drop my eyes, "should we discuss your parent's funeral arrangements?"

Ke'ain seems confused at my question at first. I assume his translator chip is attempting to catch up.

"Funerals." Ke'ain taps the side of his head where his chip would be implanted. "Fi'len don't have funerals, Opal. Their bodies were immediately returned to the sacred waters. We will honor them by living as happily as we can."

"I'll do my best. We've got lots of preparations for your coronation once we get back, I assume."

"What preparations would be made? After the wedding, I'll be crowned and so will you."

The fi'len are anything if not an expedient and practical species—I've always hated funerals anyway.

"This is some wedding dress," I tell one of my attendants as she ties shut the green gossamer robe. It is completely sheer, and I have no coverage of any kind underneath.

I blush as I look at how big my bush has gotten. Jesus, what I wouldn't give for a cheap razor to tidy up a bit. I wonder what kind of grooming the fi'len do... I mean, the only hair Ke'ain has is on his head. Maybe they think I'm some kind of hairy freak. The idea is laughable to me. I might be rocking one lofty bush, but my leg and arm hair is so light blonde that I rarely shaved it back home.

I part the robe and frown. "Should I, you know, shave before the ceremony?"

"You should go into the ceremony as the goddess made you. Is it human tradition to remove your crotch mane?" the eldest of the group asks me matter-of-factly.

I push my hand over my mouth to stifle a snicker. Jesus Christ—*crotch mane*? "Well, it's personal preference. Some sexual partners don't mind, but some prefer it hairless. They find it cleaner."

"You are the future queen, if you wish to remove your crotch mane, we can assist you. I do not think King Ke'ain finds any fault in your current state though."

"Oh my god, I wasn't asking for help. I assure you if I decide to remove my, um, crotch mane, I can do it solo. But if you think it's fine as is, I probably shouldn't chance the razor burn, should I?"

"Even though you're not fi'len, the goddess will want you as you are. Your human goddess surely gave you hair there for a reason; let's assume she'd want you to keep it." The leader of the attendants smiles as she grabs an ornate beaded headpiece from the dressing table.

The headpiece has a tall row of long, golden pointed shells. The shells are nestled into a cap of emeralds. Their raw edges, jagged and beautiful, remind me of the dark sand beaches of this planet. The attendant places the half-moon shaped diadem onto my coiffed and bouncy curls, tilting it forward so the shell spikes point true north. She ties a bow at the nape of my neck to hold the piece in place.

As the attendant steps back and I appraise my reflection, I'm stunned. If I could take away my shyness over my nudity, I would think I am some old fairy-tale beauty. I am drop-dead gorgeous and glad that the royal color of the fi'len suits my skin tone so well. The green of the emeralds and my dress bring out the rosy lips and cheeks my nervousness must have inspired.

"Thank you," I say before placing a hand on each attendant's shoulder as they bow and exit.

"The king will be with you shortly, madam," the last attendant says to me.

Before she makes her way out of the door, I ask, "Is it bad luck here for the king to see me before the wedding?"

"No?"

"Okay, thank you..." I pause. I was so busy worrying about my goddamn pubic hair that I forgot to ask their names. *God, I'm going to be such a shit queen.*

"Jes'inth, my lady." She lowers her eyes as she shuts the door.

When a knock startles me from my daydream, I jolt on the chaise lounge.

"Ke'ain?" I ask.

A muffled voice speaks. "No madam, it's Al'frind. May I come in?"

I'm decent enough. "Sure."

The elderly fi'len man enters my chambers and dips into a deep bow. He's incredibly graceful for having a face so filled with wrinkles and lines. The lines somehow make his face seem even kinder.

"You look beautiful, ma'am," he says with an appraising smile.

His starched green uniform lacks the wrinkles of his skin.

"Thank you, Al'frind. Who would have thought I'd end up here?"

"Not me, that's for sure." His gaze softens. "But the goddess chooses our mates in mysterious ways, I suppose."

Al'frind gestures to the space beside me. I pat the seat beside me, encouraging him to sit.

"You're good for him, and I think you'll be good for the realm. We need a grounding force for the monarchy. I loved Ke'ain's father," his eyes mist with memories, "but greed ruled him in the end. I know that won't happen to Ke'ain. With you to love, I don't think he'd even care about all the credits in the universe." He places a hand on my leg, leaving a small black box there.

"Is this for me, Al'frind?" I ask, palming the box and inspecting the little gift.

"Indeed, it was Ke'ain's mother's—there's no one more fitting than the future queen to have it now."

I crack open the lid and sparkling light hits one of the most brilliant emeralds I've ever seen. It's set into a bracelet made of the tiniest little black links. I assumed they would be metal given their size, but on closer inspection, they are made of the same stone as the box.

"It's beautiful, thank you."

"You're welcome, ma'am." He smirks before assuming his normal stiff posture. "I gave it to Ke'ain's mother the day he was born; it was my mate's bracelet before that."

I pull the bracelet to my chest, my eyes watering.

"Promise me you'll take good care of him. I won't be here forever to keep him out of harm's way," the regal fi'len says.

"I'll do my best," I whisper. "You really love him, don't you, Al'frind?"

"He came into this world the day after my mate died." He frowns. "A horrible virus swept the planet, and unfortunately, Jas'yrn and our unborn child didn't survive."

His voice might not reflect sadness, but I know self-preservation when I see it. After my parents died, sometimes numbness was the easier option.

"I'm so sorry."

"Ke'ain gave me something to live for when I didn't think I could go on. It's been my most humble honor to be his butler, his teacher."

I stand and open my arms to the kind alien.

"Now, that wouldn't be proper, madam. I'll see you both after the wedding." The fi'len leaves the room without giving me time to respond.

I slip the bracelet over my wrist, and the links shrink to fit my much smaller proportions.

I will treasure this gift.

☆KE'AIN

I didn't know what my mate would look like. I would dream of meeting her. I'd think of how she was built for me. I'd know true happiness when I came inside her perfect cunt. I'd wax poetic on her features, how she was the most beautiful mate I'd ever seen. Then I would wake up, and not be able to recall my dream mate in my mind's eye.

It's a good thing I can't remember, because nothing would

compare to the beauty who stands before me. Opal's pink form fills out the ceremonial gown in ways a fi'len woman could never. The curves of her body, the softness and warmth of her midsection, and the swollen pillows of her breasts tipped with a darker pink nipple. My mouth waters as I imagine myself taking her nipple between my lips in the temple. How it will be no challenge to complete our wedding ceremony.

"You're...you're..." I don't know what words I could say to convey how beautiful she is as she stands before me.

"Do I look alright, babe?" Opal does a little spin, as if to show off her green robe.

"I can't believe you're mine forever." I walk toward her, tipping her chin up to my lips with a finger.

She pushes to her tiptoes and kisses me softly.

"I feel like I'm getting the better end of the deal there, bud. You sure it's alright—this doesn't leave much to the imagination, does it?" She runs her hands up her hips and grins playfully. "You know, I would have thought your religion would be a bit more conservative."

"You have nothing to be ashamed about. Your body is beautiful," I say proudly.

"Ke'ain, I figured you'd think I had it going on when you walked through here in a sheer robe too." She laughs, taking her hand and dragging it against the sensitive flesh of my cock. "I can even see my favorite sucker." She winks as she pinches her favorite thing.

I, King of Sontafrul 6, moan in a way unbecoming of a king.

"The monarchy is conservative, but our religion celebrates the fi'len form," I say, trying to regain my composure.

"Think they could be alright with the human form?"

"They'll be jealous of that perfect form, if anything." I smile and kiss her again.

"Let's save it for tonight, big boy. I can even play a born again virgin if you want." Opal pushes on my chest and waggles her brows at me.

"Why would I want you to pretend to be a virgin?" I'm dumbfounded at her suggestion.

"Fuck, I love Sontafrul 6!" She raises her arms into the air. "I get to have a full bush and not have to pander to human male fantasies...this is heaven!"

"You'll pander to no one's fantasies but mine, I hope." I frown, unsure of what human men have to do with anything. I am happy to "save some for later," but human wedding ceremonies must be very different from fi'len. Surely, the attendants informed her of the rites. I am sure they are very different from her own.

"Of course Ke'ain, I'm yours." She grabs my hand. "Now and forever."

"And I am yours. Shall we make our way to the temple?"

"I can't wait," she says.

Putting my arm around the small of her back, I guide her to the door. As we pass the bureau, I realize I nearly forgot to grab the gags.

Goddess, how embarrassing would that be to arrive at the wedding without gags?

☆OPAL

He's perfect. His ripped swimmer's body flexes beneath his sheer robe. Even his cock is beautiful. I giggle, realizing he's in the midst of popping a boner. I guess my husband can't handle a little sucker play, can he? I can't wait to find all the sensitive spots on his body. *I promise to make it my queenly duty to learn all the spots that give you pleasure,* I vow silently to Ke'ain.

He holds two strips of green fabric in the hand that isn't holding mine. I wonder if maybe the fi'len do a handfasting of sorts—I always thought that to be a beautiful ceremony. There's a surprising amount of pagans in the Midwest who work food service, so I'd gotten to see it several times.

My own parents had a courthouse wedding to quell the

rumor mill before they had me, a ten pound "preemie." I wouldn't be surprised if my pawpaw held a shotgun the entire time. It may sound morose, but it was strangely comforting knowing that neither of our parents would be attending. It made the sting of their loss a tiny bit more manageable to know that we were both in this together.

Ke'ain drags me down a series of halls and steps. This path is obviously one that he knows well. I don't pay attention to the directions we take. I mostly just stare at his face. Love feels so great. I didn't think it would feel like this—it feels *safe*.

Ke'ain stops before a pair of doors that seem carved of ebony. They tower over even Ke'ain and have a foreboding presence.

"Opal May Legare, will you marry me?" He strokes the side of my face with the back of his hand.

"Of course." I melt into Ke'ain's touch; I am his.

Ke'ain pushes the doors, and they swing open with a squeak from their ancient hinges. They part, revealing a huge cavern. Huge emerald stalactites cover the walls and ceiling of the cavern. The floor houses a series of steps, and pools of water swarm with some kind of blue light. The sides of the room are filled with a crowd of people, all standing and staring at us. They extend their hands toward us and hum a low note.

The noise of so many soft voices triggers something strange inside me, and a feeling of relaxation fills my chest. I step through the door frame, reaching toward the people that stand here to witness our wedding. I feel Ke'ain's hand in front of my chest, and stop my movement into the emerald cavern.

"First you must tie this gag around me, and then I will tie yours," Ke'ain whispers. I must look dubious as Ke'ain explains further. "We must be mute before the goddess."

Oh, okay, so this is some weird religious thing then? I did say we would do the wedding in the fi'len tradition, so I suppose I should be okay with those traditions.

"Okay babe, I trust you," I say.

He gently places the green strip of fabric between my lips. I expect him to tie the fabric loosely, but I'll be damned if Ke'ain doesn't fucking give me whiplash as he ties the strip of fabric...well, like an actual fucking gag. I couldn't speak if I wanted to. He places a kiss on top of my head, and fuck, I'm already throbbing between the legs.

Am I attracted to this? Because maybe we can take the gags back to our room for some wedding night festivities. Or would that be super blasphemous? Shit, I really need a crash course on this religion. *Holy shit!* I don't even know what their religion is called.

I give Ke'ain no mercy either, and tie his gag just as tight—maybe that act is just as necessary as these sheer robes. Ke'ain takes my hand and leads me down the steps into the cavern. Our humming guests seem so reverent toward me, their voices reminding me of a cat's purr.

The glow of the pools makes everything so ethereal—my fairy princess ensemble now complete with a fitting location. We stop at the furthest pool from the doors, and as we arrive, a veiled figure beckons at us. She stands in front of the pool we now face.

Ke'ain steps into the magical pool. He turns back to me and gestures with his hand for me to join him.

The pool's water is hot tub temperature. I let out a small sigh as we slip into its welcoming warmth. It sounds ridiculous through the gag, but it feels so fucking delightful. I swear the humming from our guests, about two hundred or so I think, must be altering my mood. I am entirely euphoric.

When the veiled figure speaks, her voice is almost as melodic as a song. "You come before the goddess, before your subjects as mutes." The white-veiled fi'len woman gestures to the pool of water we're in. "Entering the sacred waters, you show the goddess that the voice of one shall not drown out the power of our voices united."

The priestess sings a series of notes, in harmony with the crowd; her voice is awe-inspiring. When she sings her last note, the crowd silences. The lack of happy noise is almost painful.

"Without each other, without our community, without the goddess, we are incomplete. You will commit to each other today; you will be unified." As she speaks, Ke'ain turns me to face him, clasps one of my hands against his chest, and presses his other hand into my chest. "After today, you will be mated for life. You come here of your own free will and accept the mate our goddess has selected for you."

Ke'ain releases my hands and takes my headpiece off, dropping it into the deeper end of the pool. He pulls my hand up to his head and signals I need to remove his headpiece as well. When I do, he motions to the opposite end of the pool with his head. I chuck his probably priceless adornment like a dirty shoe. It clips the side of the pool before ricocheting back down into the water. *I am such a klutz; thank god there's no photographer.*

"Opal, remove your mate's gag," the priestess says.

Ke'ain crouches, turning his head to the side, allowing me access to the knot. I tug, removing his gag. Ke'ain licks his lips as the fabric drops free into the waters.

"Ke'ain, remove your mate's gag."

As he leans forward, his lips brush right by my ear. "Maybe I'll gag you tonight."

I pinch his biceps and say, "You know, I think I like you better with a gag in *your* mouth."

But holy fuck, yes. I'll need to make a point to bring up the gagging when we're not in space church.

"Now, let us raise our voices again before consummation; let the new couple join our song!" The priestess speaks in a fever pitch.

"Consummate?" I whisper, confused.

Ke'ain shrugs the sheer robe from his shoulders. The fabric is pulled toward the deep end of the pool along with our other accouterments.

He motions for me to do the same. I clutch at the fabric

covering me. It may be sheer, but sheer feels a whole hell of a lot more covered than nude.

I raise my voice over the rumble of the crowd so my darling husband might better hear. "Ke'ain, we are not fucking consummating our wedding in front of *everyone!*"

CHAPTER 10

☆CHURCH FUCKING☆

☆OPAL

KE'AIN STANDS nude in front of me in the space hot tub and looks completely hurt. I've goofed big fucking time.

"Opal, you said you wanted to marry me," he whispers, embarrassed.

"Oh my god, Ke'ain, I do! Can't we just do the sex part alone?" I plead, trying my best to keep my voice hushed under the hum of the crowd.

He pulls me in by my shoulders, the warm waters rushing against my body.

"Opal, the sex part is the wedding..." He brushes a loose blond curl behind my ear. His eyes hold kindness, but there's still a deep pain behind them. "I thought you knew."

"I did not, in fact, *know*," I say through gritted teeth, "that I would have to have *public church sex* as part of the wedding."

"Well, that's the deal Opal. The marriage ceremony is the actual consummation."

I suddenly feel like the worst person alive. My rushing into this, having no idea what this wedding might entail, is ruining everything.

Hi, I'm Opal, the future ruler of a planet I know jack shit about.

"Oh." I press my hand to my mouth.

"We can stop, Opal. Maybe there's something else we can do," he says gently.

"No."

"What do you mean no?" he asks.

"Let's get to church fucking," I say with a huff.

I can do this for him; he's saved me so many times, what's a little public fornication? My pulse races, and I allow the hum of the crowd to fill me with that calming feeling again.

"Are you sure?" Ke'ain whispers. "Remember what I promised you—we'd never do anything you didn't want to do."

"And that, big boy," I say as I drop the robe into the glowing pool, "is exactly why I'm okay with this."

We're both standing nude in a pool surrounded by hundreds of humming aliens. My feet are stuck to the rough floor of the grotto, and my arms are as heavy as lead. Man, what I wouldn't give for a go-go juice shot right about now.

I won't let Ke'ain down.

My vision narrows, and a tension builds in my chest as my heart pounds and threatens to burst from my ribcage. Am I having a panic attack? Fuck!

I want to do this, dammit. I want to do it for Ke'ain. *I need to do it for my future people.* Jesus fuck, I'm spiralling. I look for something to ground me.

"I've got you," he says, wrapping his arms around me. "I've got you."

Ke'ain kisses down my throat, kneeling as his lips linger on my belly. He turns me by the hips so that I can't see anyone but him. Although I can still hear the hum of the crowd, all I can see is my Ke'ain. He kisses lower yet, and somehow the anxiety from seconds before melts into desire.

"I'm going to make sure you feel good, Opal. I want to make you feel good for the rest of your life."

Ke'ain runs one of his large fingers gently over the lips of my pussy. The warm waters of the pool combining with my nectar make me all the more slick. He rests his chin on my stomach and looks up at me as though I am his own personal deity.

"I love you, you know, so fucking much." I stroke his damp, pale hair off his forehead.

"I should hope you love me, Opal," he says before lifting me by the ass and placing me on the side of the glowing blue pool. "Because I'd hate to waste the enthusiasm of my tongue on someone who didn't."

Ke'ain lays my body on the shining green floor, his eyes roving over my pussy as if it's some splendid feast—and Ke'ain is starving for it.

"You look good enough to eat," my king says to me.

I look at my man in awe as he places his mouth on me. The lower half of his face is obscured by my flushed mound. Ke'ain is a crocodile and I am the Nile river.

His tongue works slow strokes from my entrance to my clit. As the pressure of his licking intensifies, I grab on to his white hair and arch back.

Only when I open my eyes do I remember I am surrounded by hundreds of singing aliens. For a mere moment I am ashamed —but that shame dies as my perfect alien mate sucks my clit into his eager mouth. I don't close my eyes, but take the crowd in as a whole. No one in this room besides me finds this wrong. Everyone except me knew what rituals and rites would occur today at our wedding.

I should have asked more about the planet I will help rule.

At this moment, I decide to let the puritanical parts of Earth Opal die for good. I grab Ke'ain by his cheeks and pull his face toward mine. Within seconds, his big gray body completely eclipses my own.

"Forever?" I ask, as I reach my hand down to feel his rigid cock.

"Forever," he agrees as he lets my hand guide him home.

As his massive length fills me, I feel no shame in the moan

that leaves my lips. In fact, with each stroke, I get louder. The crowd matches my enthusiasm, their hum reaching a fever pitch.

The energy from their previously calm melody now fuels our love making. Ke'ain thrusts deeper yet as he slips his hand behind my neck. He pulls me forward as he stands and brings us both back into the water. His hand under my ass helps lift me as I slide up his cock. Gravity slams me back down as he fills me again. His hips are half in the water and between our fucking and his glorious sucker, the slurping and splashing noises are obscene. I love it.

The crowd raises their arms to the ceiling of the cavern, their voices becoming a chorus of staccato breathing and yelps. As their voices rise, the top of the cavern glows the same blue of the pools. I'm in awe as I watch the blue effervescent light spread.

Ke'ain's pace becomes brutal. With every bounce, his sucker attaches and pops off my clit deliciously. The veiled priestess is speaking too fast and low for my translator chip to keep up. Honestly at that moment, not the crowd, not the priestess, not even the absolutely bonkers journey that brought me here, matters.

It's just Ke'ain and me. His fingers dig into the meat of my ass and the skin at the back of my neck. He pulls me tightly into him, his breath becoming uneven.

"I'm going to come, I'm going to fill you so deeply, Opal." His voice is muffled as he pushes his face into my neck.

"I'm so close, babe!" I pant as his sucker tugs at my clit.

I feel him grit his teeth, almost as if he's determined to make me find my release before his own. Ke'ain moves his mouth to my breast and sucks the peak into his mouth. As his teeth graze my nipple and he bites down softly, it's just enough to send me over the edge.

"You're so perfect," he mouths with eyes wide. The blue glow from the ceiling reflects and intensifies the color of his own eyes.

The crowd is almost screaming now—and the room is so brightly lit that I am forced to shut my eyes tightly.

As I arch and my pussy contracts violently around Ke'ain's length, his balls tighten, and he floods me with his load. Ke'ain's legs give out, and we slowly sink into the warm waters of the glowing pool.

Ke'ain's cock's throbbing subsides inside of me, my thighs washed in his slippery seed. We still cling to each other, and I press a bruising kiss to his lips.

Without warning, the crowd stops their song, and the cavern ceiling and the glowing pools around us go dark. The only light in the huge cave comes from the pool in which we're submerged. The veiled priestess leans forward, the light from the water letting me ever so slightly make out the shape of her face as she speaks.

"Now, you swim toward your future. Greet your kingdom." The priestess's voice cuts through the silence of the space.

Ke'ain draws a breath, cupping my face and looking at me in a way so adoring that tears threaten to crest from my eyes.

"Now we must swim through the ceremonial tunnels of my ancestors and meet our public at the surface. I will breathe for you," he says and I nod. "Just hold me tightly, Opal."

As if he had to ask.

His cock is still within me as he motions for me to take a deep breath. I do and we plunge underwater. Ke'ain holds me tightly as he kicks with his powerful legs to the far side of the pool.

I know I should shut my eyes, but I can't help but keep them open. Even though my field of vision is blurred, this underwater world is beautiful. The blue glow of the pool extends deeply into the ancestor's tunnels. Emerald green outcroppings of giant gem-like structures line the edges.

Ke'ain takes turns so quickly I feel like he's known this place his entire life. He slows only to breathe fresh air into my burning lungs.

He hardens again as our lips touch, and as he adjusts me in

his grip, I can tell he's trying not to thrust into me once more. He is an alien on a mission, and I should probably quit flexing my inner muscles, but I can't help it.

I know I'm fucked on my good behavior when Ke'ain's sucker grips onto to my swollen clit. I lift my hips as we propel through the water.

As I push myself back down and his sucker grabs its target again, Ke'ain stops kicking.

My alien moans, bubbles leaving his mouth as he pushes me up against a smoother section of the emerald walls.

"Never satisfied, little Opal?" He smirks, and the water distorts his voice, but it's still that of my husband.

I smile but don't speak, not wanting to waste the air in my lungs. He pushes my hips against the wall and draws slowly out of me. The weightlessness of being underwater lets Ke'ain's cock hit an angle that makes me shudder with pleasure. He hits my G-spot once more as he thrusts again. This time I let a moan escape my lips. The precious air in my lungs escapes only to have Ke'ain push fresh air into them once more.

He places one large hand onto my midsection, its width nearly covering my entire waist. As he fucks me, he moves his other hand to play with my clit. His cock doesn't fill me completely at the angle in which he works, and just because his sucker is amazing doesn't mean I don't love it as his hand slides up and down the sensitive nerve endings.

Bubbles float from my lips as I cry out again as he rolls the nub between his fingers. His cock hits home as it pounds my G-spot relentlessly.

Is it squirting if you're underwater?

I realize my lungs are burning, my last gasp emptying them of oxygen. I look toward a blurry Ke'ain. Even with my limited vision, I can tell that is the face of a man about to come.

The throbbing of my pussy supersedes the nagging of my chest.

I shudder as my already overstimulated body is pushed over

the edge once more. I can't tell if the orgasm is just that strong, or maybe it's the lack of oxygen, but I don't think I've ever come so hard.

Ke'ain whispers something, but I'm too busy floating into darkness—black spots fill my peripherals. Ke'ain lips bring sweet oxygen into my mouth, and I breathe it in greedily. I ragdoll against him, my body boneless. He pulls me from the wall and we continue on our journey. I close my eyes now, my energy completely gone.

It's only when we crest the waters do I open my eyes to bright sunlight.

CHAPTER 11
☆HOME☆

☆OPAL

IT TAKES a moment for my eyes to adjust. The sunlight streaming through the glass dome we've surfaced into is blinding after winding our way through the ceremonial tunnels.

I draw a huge breath as I'm able to taste fresh air. Ke'ain releases me for the first time since the wedding ceremony to pull his own body out of the water. The way the water droplets sluice down his muscled back has me subconsciously biting my lip. He turns to me and extends a hand.

I'm pulled from the effervescent waters into the warm receiving room. Frosted glass covers every surface, including the double doors at its entrance. My eyes fall onto two ornate robes made of stiff dark green fabric that are arranged artfully on mannequins. Their structural shapes seem to be held rigid by the gold wires woven through the fabric into beautiful geometric designs. Their look feels vaguely Art Deco, but decidedly alien. Beside the robes lay two headpieces done in the same style. Their shape is almost like that of the hat the pope wears.

Maybe the weirdos on that Ancient Aliens *TV show have more merit than I thought.*

Ke'ain grabs one of the lush folded towels and drapes it over my shoulders. He rubs my biceps through the towel to dry me.

"Human skin holds onto so much water compared to mine," he muses lovingly. He pushes the towel up to my hair and jostles my strands a bit too roughly. "And your mane, it stays wet forever. I should have had them bring a heater, Opal. I'm sorry I've been so inconsiderate."

"Are you kidding me, Ke'ain?" I laugh. "You are one of the most considerate beings I've ever met. Like honestly, you've just been *very* considerate, twice, so cool your jets, *Sharkboy*."

"I suppose I should just consider that a term of endearment at this point?" Ke'ain chuckles.

I make a mental note to never tell him about Lavagirl. I don't want to encourage any cringe nicknames on my end.

"I'm sorry I wasn't better prepared for what just happened." My voice is muffled as he continues to rub the towel over my head.

"No, I should have taken more time to explain things to you. Or at the very least had the attendants explain things to you." He pulls the towel from my face and grabs the smaller gown from its dress form.

I spin around, giving him my arm as he holds the robe open. I slide it into the sleeve and wiggle into its warmth. It's incredibly structured, and its balloon shape has me feeling a bit like a Fabergé egg, but it's so warm I don't mind.

Hell, after fornicating in an alien church, there's not much I mind anymore.

Ke'ain dons his own robe, placing the headpiece on his white hair. For as silly as I'm sure I look, he looks entirely regal.

"Are you ready to greet your kingdom, Opal?" he says, taking my hand and placing it into the crook of his elbow.

I nod as we make our way toward the frosted glass doors, the chatter of the crowd behind them.

"Do you think they'll like me?" I ask, suddenly nervous to

see the people I'll be responsible for. My palms feel clammy on the scratchy fabric of Ke'ain's robe.

"They'll respect you, as their queen. That's what you need from them, because I'll give you all the love you'll need."

He's right. I feel like I can do anything with this man's unconditional love. I hope I can give him back even a fraction of what he's given me.

I step forward and push open the doors.

It's like stepping into a different reality as I cross the threshold. Thousands of fi'len and other aliens fill my field of vision. They wave banners of emerald and gold. Aliens of all shapes, sizes and colors smile and cheer...No, not aliens, my people.

My public.

My family.

For the first time since my parents died, I feel like I'm *home*.

☆KE'AIN

We're rushed into my silver cruiser by the king's guard at the conclusion of our royal procession. Opal is finally my wife, my *queen*.

Despite our miscommunication, of which I'm sure we will have many more, she followed through her portion of the ceremony perfectly. Humans seem so private with their affections; I imagine she must have had to be very brave to share her love so publicly.

The ancient crowns of the Sontafrul 6 monarchy adorn our heads. Opal's petite form swims in her ceremonial garb—the antique robe made for my ancestors' larger bodies.

I look at her now, sitting next to me in the same cruiser I first saw her in—she beams with pride, with love, with a regalness I've not seen from my paramour before.

"Are you happy?" I ask as she settles her shoulders into the plush upholstery of the cruiser's seats.

She places her small pink palm on my thigh and nuzzles my head into her side.

"I haven't been this happy in a long time," she says, her eyelids heavy.

"I'm glad we've secured your place here, Opal. Things might become treacherous as we plan our assault on the Deenz."

As my beautiful bride's euphoric face drops, I wish I had waited until tomorrow to bring up our enemy.

"Oh, yeah, the Deenz." She frowns, looking up at me, "Is it bad that I forgot about them?"

"I wish I could forget about them too, but I won't rest until you're safe. I'm just so confused why they would sell your contract and then try to harm you?"

"Fuck if I know, babe." She sighs, removing the oversized crown from her brow. "I do know that regardless of why they want me back, I can't let them keep taking girls from Earth. Not every gal will meet a Ke'ain to protect her from the hive-minded idiots."

"Oh, the other women…"

My jaw sets contemplatively. I hadn't thought far enough ahead to figure out what we'd do with all the humans that would be displaced after we defeated their captors.

"How many do you think there are? There were at least forty on the bus with me."

"Forty on your bus, a bus at every club on Sontafrul 6, and repeat that by an exponential number of planets in this solar system alone…There are going to be so many human refugees if we win this fight."

"*We* can guarantee them a safe place here, can't we? I can't just leave my fellow Earthlings to rot."

I don't want to say no. Opal's eyes do that thing where they turn into shiny orbs and her bottom lip pouts out at a strange angle. It is human witchcraft, I'm sure.

"We can help some of them, but I'm not sure about *all*—"

"This is non-negotiable. If they can make it here, we will make a home for them."

"'I tried,' I'll tell my council, 'but your queen *pouted.'* I am under your thumb, and I don't mind one bit." She rolls her eyes as I feign, only partly, my subservience to my beautiful wife.

"So, let's deal with the Deenz tomorrow. Tonight I'd like to just enjoy my husband." Opal winks.

"Have you not been enjoying him already today?" I clutch my chest. The longer I'm with Opal, the more I enjoy teasing her.

She bats at my chest and chuckles.

"I'm looking forward to a good night's rest. You know, I don't quite remember the last time I had a decent night's sleep." She yawns.

"That's *another* thing I should have spoken to you about," I say as I stroke her hair.

She arches an eyebrow at me. "What other surprises await me today?"

"We aren't going home. We're to spend the night in the original palace and sleep as the first monarchs did." I can feel her body stiffen.

"How weirdly did they sleep, Ke'ain? Please tell me weird for the fi'len just means a down filled bed…"

"We'll sleep in the waters of I'loh tonight. It's tradition and is supposed to," I cough, trying to stifle the last bit of information I need to impart, "increase the chances of conception."

"Ke'ain, for one thing, who even knows if our reproductive systems line up in that way. Two, humans aren't meant to sleep in water…" She seems exhausted suddenly.

"I promise you, we'll figure it out on both accounts, Opal."

"You want lil ole me to have your possibly huge babies?" She gestures to her stomach. "I've only got room for food babies right now, bud. Let's take care of the Deenz, and we'll worry about how cute our babies are after humans are a bit safer round these parts."

I look at her soft belly and imagine her with my child. Maybe

I'm naïve, but with how well we fit together, I assume the chances of her being pregnant are more likely than not. I'll humor her for now, but I'll find a way to make sure we get at least some rest in the waters of I'loh. Best not to anger the goddess by breaking tradition.

"I promise you a bed full of feathers after tonight, if that's what you want. This one last tradition is the last I force on you this year."

"So. Many. Feathers," Opal squeaks out as she lets her eyelids drift closed.

I wish the ride was longer so I could hold her just a bit more. But not long after Opal closes her eyes, the cruiser slows to a stop. We've arrived in front of the foreboding castle of the monarch's past. Its black Tr'ael rocks look as if their jagged structure sprung forth from the ground. A single attendant waits at the grand doorway for our arrival.

Al'frind swings open the cruiser door.

"Welcome, my king," he says, dipping into a deep bow. He eyes Opal slumbering against my chest. "Sir, I do believe the queen is drooling. May I assist you?"

He removes the white square of fabric from his jacket pocket. I chuckle, but raise a hand to dismiss his offer. I scoop up my slumbering wife and make our way into the ancient castle.

☆OPAL

I'm roused from sleep as my body slides into the warm and bubbling waters. My head jerks up and my eyes whip open to see Ke'ain's gray face smiling down at me.

"Shhh...I told you I'd help you sleep," he whispers as he cradles me in his arms.

"Ke'ain, I told you before I can't sleep in the water..." I say as he floats his big body behind mine, as if he's some kind of living pool raft. The water is the same as from our wedding—blue, glowing, and warm.

I think my alien husband can control the buoyancy of his body. I feel him adjust and Ke'ain drops his torso slightly down so that I'm enveloped in the heated liquid. My head rests in the hollow spot between his pectorals as he holds me.

I want to tell him I love him. That I treasure him so much.

Instead, I just let the gentle motion of the water rock me back into sleep.

Home.

CHAPTER 12
# ☆PERSONAL SPACE IN OUTER SPACE☆

☆OPAL

I SEEM to drift in and out of sleep. One second I'm in the warm waters of the alien hot tub and the next thing I know, I'm being cradled by my big alien husband.

"Ke'ain—" I whisper as I peek from beneath my eyelids.

"Shhh, Opal, get some more sleep. You're exhausted," he says as he kisses my forehead.

"Are we going home?" I ask, still thick with the confusion of sleep.

"We're still in the old palace, but I had Al'frind bring a feather bed here for you." He pushes through a doorway into a massive, darkly lit chamber. This entire building is made of the same ebony rock I've seen in smaller applications at the new palace.

The room is foreboding, all sharp edges and angles. For a second I'm worried, but that's only until Ke'ain lays my head onto what might be the softest thing I've ever set these old bones down on.

"Jesus fuck, is there some kind of alien angel you skinned to get something this soft?" I coo.

Ke'ain cocks his head. "We don't have angels here, although the wings must be quite impressive to behold."

I roll my eyes when I realize his translator chip must have shown him a painting of the archangel Michael and that aliens probably don't subscribe to Christianity.

"But these are feathers from the ckra'rot, and they are quite difficult to get." He pulls a soft blanket up to my chin.

"Aren't you gonna join me for some married snuggles?" I frown, realizing he's already dressed in his formal green suit.

"I will meet with the war committee to discuss our first move against the Deenz and how best to acclimate our human refugees."

I bolt upright. "Without me?" I ask, a little hurt.

"You're joining me tomorrow morning. The sun is almost setting now—you've slept through most of the day, Opal. We can start anew in the morning if you give me some peace of mind and just a few more hours of sleep. You need some recovery time. The rituals pushed you too far yesterday."

He presses my shoulders back into the deliciously soft bed.

"I want you to know, this is your one freebie on telling me what to do—and you're lucky this bed is so damn nice...." My eyelids drift closed against my better judgment.

"Noted," Ke'ain says as he makes his way toward the chamber doors. "I have some tailors coming in a bit for your new wardrobe as well. I've instructed Al'frind to allow them up once you're ready."

"Oh, what should I get made? What does a queen wear?" I'm suddenly nervous again about my new position.

"What does a queen wear? Whatever she wants, Opal."

God damn, do I love this man. The door closes with a soft click, and I fall back asleep.

☆KE'AIN

I don't want to leave her at the old palace, nor do I ever want to leave her alone. But given our positions, we'll need to be in different castles eventually. I feel safe leaving her with Al'frind, in any case. He's been with me since the day I was born. There is only one other I trust as much as him—Gra'eth.

As I step into the cruiser, I say, "Make sure she's safe, Al'frind. Call me if anything comes up."

"The queen, and the king, will always be my priority," he says as he clicks the silver door shut. "I know what she means to you, and you know what she means to me as my queen."

I sigh and thank the goddess I have him. Even with the occasional snark and pomp that seems to come with his role, he's always wanted the best for me. He's like the father I always wanted.

I place my hand on the window glass as we pull away.

Just a few more hours, and I'll be back in her arms. I don't think I ever truly understood our people's mate bond until I felt it myself. Every atom inside my body calls to her. Every piece feels incomplete without that silly human woman.

☆OPAL

I'm awake, but my eyes don't want to open. They're as heavy as a lead jacket. My arms and thighs ache as my recent adventures catch up with me. Who'd have thought a Kentucky gal like me would end up here?

I should get up, put on my big girl panties, and learn how to be a monarch—but goddamn, this bed is the best thing I've ever felt. I mean, besides Ke'ain's tongue, fingers, and cock…

Oh no, I should be getting up… not getting off. Despite that though, my hand drifts between my legs. *Well fuck, I might as well have a little self-care time, right?*

I wish Ke'ain could have stayed a bit longer. I think about

how good it felt to sit on his face as he worked my clit with his tongue. My hand presses into the wetness beading on my pussy. I dip my index finger deep and spread the slickness. I work the fingertip in slow, small circles at the part that aches the most.

My finger slips easily over my clit and sends sparks down to my toes.

God, I wish Ke'ain were here. He treats my pleasure like it's a prize he gets for good behavior. Of all the planets in the universe I could have ended up on, I must have done something right to end up on this one with him.

I pluck at my clit in a tragic attempt to recreate his glorious sucker. It's no substitute, so I switch tactics.

I wet my hand again and pull back my folds with the other. I stroke my fingers quickly over the engorged bud, imagining my big gray husband taking my nipple greedily into his mouth.

My pace becomes frantic as I work my hand faster still, my legs and ass tightening as I approach the crest.

I feel my pussy pulse as I finally hit the summit, its muscles contracting in waves of pleasure as I palm the sensitive nerves and try my best to ride out the orgasm as it rockets through my body.

What I wouldn't give to have Ke'ain lick my hand and tell me I'm a good girl.

I slow the pace of my breathing and wipe my hand on my stomach. I don't know how much this mattress cost, but it feels wrong to wipe my cum on it. This shit feels expensive.

So here I lay, Opal, queen of forethought, realizing I have no idea where the bathroom or my clothing might be. I guess my pussy literally comes first, right?

I wrap the blanket tightly around my body and make my way toward the door. It takes more muscles than I want to admit to move it. The giant black stone door doesn't want to open, but I get it eventually.

I peek into the hallway, and Al'frind's stiffly buttoned suit jacket immediately greets me.. His chest practically stops my nose.

"Oh hi, Al'frind!, I don't have any clothing…do you know where I might get some? I know the tailors are coming soon, but I—"

I look at his face, and his mouth is twisted into a painted frown. His eyes are wet with tears that threaten to spill.

"Milady, close the door," he whispers through gritted teeth. His face is taut with fear.

I reach for his shoulder and realize his hands are behind his back.

"Al'frind, are you all right?" I ask, concerned.

"I'm so sorry, my queen. If you see the king again, tell him I tried," the old man says as he attempts to throw his weight behind him.

A purple hand snakes up under his arm, putting a blaster right to his chest, and the slimy hand pulls the trigger. Al'frind's chest explodes in a flash of gray flesh and blinding light.

The sound of the blaster burns my eardrums. As the purple hand shoots him, despite nearly destroying his entire chest, Al'frind swings his body backward. He's trying to use his larger size to pin the Deenz behind him. *His last act in this universe is to help me.*

Somehow, despite the shock settling into me, I shove my body against the door frame, but the door stops short of shutting as the stone clangs against the metal of a blaster. I shuffle backward, tripping over a side table, and fly ass over tits. My shoulder connects roughly with the stone floor, but adrenaline lets me use that shoulder despite the pain to push myself up.

"Human, you're coming with us," the purple bastard screeches as he pushes through the narrow crack in the door.

From my seated position, I shuffle backward until I hit a wall. I bring a hand to the wetness spreading across my face. Al'frind's blue blood and chunks of flesh paint my cheeks.

"You killed him…." I whisper.

Three more Deenz push open the heavy door, their hands leaving thick purple secretions everywhere they touch. *I hate them.*

I search desperately looking something to defend myself. The room is sparse except for the bed, as if the space has been empty for many years.

"Don't you come any closer!" I scream, grabbing the blanket and pulling it tighter around my body. "The king will fucking rip you limb from limb if you touch me."

More Deenz push into the room. They all look at me with blasters pointed in my direction.

"Come with us," the c twenty or so little purple aliens say in unison.

"Fuck off and die, you pieces of shit," I spit. "Why me? Can't you just leave me alone—you sold me to Ke'ain!"

The Deenz don't look at each other, but they're communicating somehow. *The hive-minded bastards have a plan.*

CHAPTER 13
FUCKING MAGNETS, HOW DO THEY WORK?

☆OPAL

ONE OF THE dripping purple Deenz steps away from the crowd and closer to me. My back is against the wall, but I kick my legs at his body as he gets closer.

"Why you?" He mocks me and points a finger squarely at my chest. "I have no idea. We didn't think a prince of Sontafrul 6 would wed a human whore." He holsters his blaster into his utility belt. "We thought he'd get his fill of your human cunt and toss you aside. We were waiting outside the palace, ready to collect you that first night."

I bite the inside of my lip. Will these bastards finally kill me here? Right after I was so sure I'd found my home?

"When he didn't toss you out, as all the others had done with the human merchandise before, we tried to break into the palace and return you to the hive. As I'm sure you're aware, that was a less than satisfactory outcome for us." His words buzz unnaturally in my ear, the Deenz accent almost mechanical.

My first night here, the harken gas, the panic room…How could they think Ke'ain would toss me out like a piece of garbage?

145

Like all the times before?

Oh god, they must have whored out human women count-less times.

"We can't have the word get back to the Universal Governing Senate that our human merchandise is less than willing. Why do you think we pump you full of hormones before your perfor-mances? Those shots aren't cheap, but we need you to appear willing and enthusiastic. Slavery is outlawed by Universal Governing Senate."

"So why wouldn't you just pump me full of harken gas so I wouldn't remember?" I ask incredulously. A blank slate would be easier to control, would it not?

"Although harken gas might work on other species in the galaxy, the effects on humans are sadly temporary. It's simply not cost-effective for us to keep pumping you full of harken gas."

"All of this suffering because you asshats are too cheap?" I screech.

"We must remain cost-effective for the hive to survive. The hive comes before everything, even your ridiculous human comfort. It's the same reason you're coming with us now," he says, pulling a restraint from his belt.

I flinch. I won't be put in cuffs again. The panic builds in my chest like an atomic bomb. I will take them all out if I have to.

"You might as well kill me now, you fucker; I'm not going quietly."

"Stupid, selfish human, I can't kill you until we get back to the hive for processing. We can't waste the investment made in you so quickly. Your organs and meats will be sold to the highest bidders on the black market. Many species love the taste of humans in the kitchen, not just the bedroom. You should be honored to be considered such a delicacy."

My body springs out from the wall before I even realize what I'm doing, and I'm on his purple scaled body like a rabid spider monkey. I bite into his neck as the bitter and stinging skin excretions fill my mouth. When the Deenz pulls back and screams, I knock my elbow directly into his sternum. The bone cracks like he's part chicken, and I spit in his face as he crumples to the ground.

"You're not fucking eating me, you bitch!" I bark.

Somewhere in my rage, I feel a sharp pain in my neck. One of the Deenz has snuck up to my side and pressed a syringe into my jugular.

"We have no taste for humans. It'll be simple enough for us not to take a bite—unlike the heathen you are," a pair of purple lips whispers into my ear.

Blackness creeps over my vision as what I'm sure would have been my best comeback yet is cut short.

"Opal, are you all right?" The woman's voice is fuzzy, and I flinch as I feel a hand touch my brow. "Calm down, peaches. It's Jessy—you remember me, don't ya?"

I feel the hard plastic seat under my ass and smell the stale scent of sweat and masturbating. Oh god, I'm back on the bus.

I jerk upright, my whole body rigid as I finally regain control of my faculties. As I try to clutch my hands to my body, they strain against the cuffs. I've been chained to the seat in front of me.

"Jessy?" My mouth feels full of cotton, and my arms feel like dead weight.

"Yeah, it's Jessy. We've met before, remember?" She strokes my brow in an attempt to comfort me. "I didn't think we'd see you again after the big gray guy took you. Are you all right? I hope he wasn't too rough with you...sometimes they're not very nice." Her eyes get distant.

I shake my head. "No, you don't understand. I married him, Jessy. The Deenz fucking kidnapped me for a second goddamn time." My face is flushed with anger, and my head lolls side to side as the bus moves.

"Sweetie, he dumped you back with us. That's what they said when they brought you back in. Judging from the bruises on your neck, you're better off here."

She's gotta be fucking confused.

"Dumped?? Why the fuck would they cuff me, then?" I ask.

"They said you were drugged, that you'd wake up angry... you really married that gray guy?" She seems shocked.

"They're going to butcher me and sell me as some human fucking delicacy, Jessy. You have to help me," I beg. I try my best to whisper, but it escapes my lips as more of a quiet shout.

Maybe more of an actual shout, because the human women in front of us turn around with their eyes wide.

"They're going to *eat* you?" a tall brunette asks.

"No way, that's such bullshit. She's high, remember?" The tall woman with an Eastern European look and a thick accent next to her says.

A chorus of hushed questions begins on the bus, and the anxiety ramps.

"I'm not fucking lying. Ke'ain, the big gray guy, he's my husband. The Deenz stole me back. They don't want the other aliens to know that they *kidnapped* us from Earth. These aliens think it's some great honor to be here. That we fight and jockey for the opportunity!" I say to the frightened crowd of thirty or so women. "Help me get out of these cuffs, and if we can get off this bus, I promise you I'll make sure you're all safe."

"How are you going to do that?" one of the other women asks.

"The big gray guy, my husband, is the king of this planet. I'm the queen. You have to believe me!" I'm begging them for help at this point. How much of their trust has been lost in their abduction trauma?

"If you're the *queen*, where's the calvary, babe?" A valley girl's voice floats over the gasps of shock and disbelief.

The bus lurches forward as something slams into the bus's bumper. The Deenz driver swivels his disgusting dripping head around and slams his foot on the gas.

"That cavalry?" I say, pushing my cuffed hands toward the crowd. "Please, we can escape if you all help me!"

Jessy is the first to grab my wrists. "Right! So I've seen this mechanism before. They use magnets to lock and unlock them."

Her face differs from what I've seen before. The former rocket scientist sticks her tongue slightly out of her mouth as she holds my wrists prone.

"Girls, this will suck, but I need you to kick the small panels under the window. That's where they house the large magnets that keep this bus afloat. If we remove them, we can disable the mag systems for the bus and break these cuffs."

Jessy turns and faces the window. She grips her hands on the handlebar near the ceiling and swings her bare feet into the metal panel. They land with a thud that sounds painful, and she winces.

She doesn't stop and kicks it again. "Girls, come on, I can't do it myself!"

The panel begins to give despite the blood left by her feet. She takes a deep breath and hits the flesh to metal once more.

Two more girls start the painful work as something rams hard into the bus again, making us swerve dangerously close to the edge of the mag lane. The Deenz driver swears and increases his speed even more. He scrapes the side of another vehicle as he pushes it from the flow of traffic. I crane my head and watch as the displaced vehicle plummets to the ground.

I turn to Jessy and see that she's gotten her panel pried open enough to reach her hand in. She's armpit deep behind the sheet metal, gritting her teeth. The muscles in Jessy's neck strain as she rips a chunk of machinery out. When she pulls the magnet from its housing, the bus wiggles slightly. As if the Deenz thinks it's another ramming attempt, we fly even faster through the air.

Jessy places the long magnet against my cuffs, and they release quickly. I pull my hands up and rub the raw red wrists.

"Thank you," I tell Jessy, who nods.

We move to the seat directly in front of us and slam our combined body weight into the panel until it gives. Jessy removes another magnet bar, and the bus drops lower in the sky.

"I got it!" I hear the tall brunette say triumphantly as she holds the magnet in the air.

"Me too—"

The bus is slammed again, but it drops from the mag lane and begins to spin. All the women are pushed to the back of the bus on the initial spin and held prone by the g-force and the crush of the other women's bodies. I can't keep my bearings about me as the spin quickens.

I fear I might vomit just as the nose of the bus crashes into something. It's almost like the world is in slow motion as I watch the Deenz burst into a mass of purple chunks. For a second I think it's snowing, but I realize quickly that it's the glass shattering.

Chunks of glass spray toward us, and I raise my forearms to protect my eyes. Before the glass can hit, the bus teeters backwards and falls. Our bodies tumble to the roof of the bus, and I reach toward Jessy for stability as the vehicle slams into the icy water. The pressure smashes all the remaining windows running along the sides, allowing the sea to flood the bus. I take several deep breaths and wait for the inevitable.

At least I won't die a slave.

At least we gave it our all.

☆ GRA'ETH

I watch in horror as the transport unit that carries my queen and my best friend's mate crashes into the tourist docks head-first. My heart stops as it tips backward into the sea.

"Fucking get down there now!" I scream to the driver of the tactical cruiser.

The jets roar to life and shake the whole vehicle as we increase our speed.

"What's happening?" From my communicator, Ke'ain's terrified voice fills my ear.

☆KE'AIN

My heart shatters into a thousand pieces as Gra'eth speaks...

"The transport unit has crashed into the sea... it's sinking fast." The words stick in his throat.

"Where?" I whisper.

"The tourist docks."

I rush to the front of the tactical vehicle. Gra'eth isn't far ahead of me, but every second counts. I push the pilot from his seat and press my hand on the throttle until it reaches the hilt—the tactical cruiser slams into motion, and my body is braced against the seat.

I will make it in time, and I will save Opal.

☆GRA'ETH

I drop from the pod bay of the tactical cruiser and land roughly on the paved road beneath me. The hover jets blow dust and debris into the crowds of tourists. The aliens who vacation on our planet gape at me. An alien child drops its chilled cr'uhn onto the ground and cries. The fi'len who runs the shops and vendors along the dock and boardwalk stares at the bus as it sinks into the waves.

I rip off my suit jacket and shoes. "Your queen and her kind are in that transport. Humans can't breathe underwater, and if you ever have had a love for your king, I urge you to help me save them now."

My people, and the variety of tourist aliens, stare at me in disbelief. I run to the edge of the dock and dive into the cold waters. I can't wait for their help.

The waters off the dock are deep and murky with debris from the transport unit. Glass shards float all around me, and the current takes a purple finger straight past my head. I hope for the Deenz's sake that's all that's left of him.

Propelling forward through the water, I wedge my body into one of the narrow broken windows. The shards of glass cut my skin, and my blue blood mists around me in the water.

I pick out a pale yellow curl in the crowd of floating human women. Opal.

I push the body in front of hers, one with hair like fire, aside to get a better grip on my queen.

The red-haired woman's eyes flash open for a moment. A bubble escapes her rosebud mouth, and she clutches at her chest. I secure Opal under my arm and am about to kick them off the wall and back into open water when I realize that this will be the other woman's last moment alive.

I can't leave her.

I grip her around the chest and pull her in, pressing my lips to hers. I give her fresh air, and she pulls it in deeply. I try not to think about all the parasites we might be exchanging as I do.

She tastes like cinnamon.

I turn to my queen and push air into her lungs as well…she doesn't respond. Her chest rises and falls, but she is limp in my arms.

I have to get Opal to the surface now.

I push both human women through the window and squeeze my shoulders through the jagged opening again. The transport unit is descending quickly, and for a moment, I'm distraught I can't save them all.

Flashes of gray fill my peripherals. It must be the fi'len on the docks. They're diving with me; we can save them.

"Give them air!" I scream to my brothers as I ascend.

A dozen fi'len bodies cut through the current. Our bodies are so well designed for the water yet so rarely in it anymore. It's a beautiful sight to behold, even if it's a rescue mission.

I'm relieved as I break the water's surface with the humans under my arms. The redhead sputters water from her lungs, but my queen is still.

Two fi'len men grab the women and pull them up on the dock so I can lift my body up. The redhead stumbles and sputters, reaching for me.

"You...you saved me," she says, shocked.

"Take a deep breath, human," I say, letting her lean into my chest. I put my arm around her. Her body is so cold, and it shakes violently as she coughs.

I push our way through the crowd that surrounds my queen as she lies motionless on the ground. When we arrive at the front, I gently set the red-haired human woman down.

The queen is nude, but a worker has thrown their jacket over her body.

"Turn her head to the side," the human says. "She's drowned. We need to get the water out of her lungs."

Drowned. The fi'len don't have such a word, but I trust her. I turn Opal's head to the side and open her mouth. The queen's lips are blue.

Through chattering teeth, the human says, "Now...now you compress her chest and try to expel the water."

She mimes pumping motions with her hands clasped over one another.

I follow her instructions and press Opal's chest. After a few compressions, nothing happens. I look toward the red-haired one again.

"Harder," she says.

"I'll break her ribs if I go much harder."

"Better a broken rib than dead," she says in a deadpan tone.

I push my whole body's weight onto her chest. With a violent cough, water pours from her lips. The queen's body seizes as she chokes on the saltwater that leaves her body.

I pull her into a sitting position and pound my fist on her back several times. Her cough is rough and sounds painful, but she's alive!

A fi'len worker hands me a blanket, and I wrap her in it, rubbing my hands up and down her arms as I try my best to warm her against my own body.

"Opal!" Ke'ain shouts as he drops from the pod bay door of his tactical cruiser. I've never seen him move so quickly as he sweeps Opal's body from my arms into his own.

"Medics!" He waves over a crew of healthcare workers.

I pull the shaking human beauty back into my arms.

"Are you all right?" I ask.

"All right is subjective," she says, "but I'm not dead. My name is Jessy." She pushes her forehead into my side and wraps her arms around me.

"I'm Gra'eth."

"Gray Seth?" she asks.

"Yes, my given name is Gray Seth," I say, although I feel my sarcasm is lost on this one.

"Thanks, Seth—for, you know, not letting me drown."

"Thank you for helping me save the queen," I whisper back.

"No shit? So Opal wasn't lying. Makes me feel a lot better about crashing the bus."

"I'm sorry, you what?"

CHAPTER 14
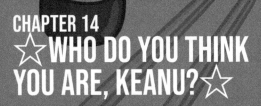 WHO DO YOU THINK YOU ARE, KEANU?

☆KE'AIN

OPAL'S SO COLD. Her blue lips are slowly regaining their color, but her freezing and bruised body is a shock to my system.

Seeing Gra'eth hovering over her lifeless body made the bile rise in my throat.

Three medics surround us, each referring to their data pads for human vitals as they check her over. Her tiny shivering hand snakes under my arm and she nuzzles her face into my chest.

"The other women," she rasps, "make sure they try and save the other women."

Opal pulls her head up, looking over my shoulder. When I turn my head, I see several fi'len men trying to clear the lungs of the other passengers on the bus. There are soldiers, food vendors, medics, and fi'len of every class helping these poor humans from what would have surely been a watery grave.

Even sarcastic and cold Gra'eth is cradling a pale red-haired human in his arms.

"They're trying, Opal." I hand her wrist to the medic beside me, and he pushes a syringe of medicine into her vein.

"Ouch, Ke'ain!" she gets out between coughs.

"No shots, I know, but this will help warm you up, Opal."

"The driver is dead, but what about the others who came for me...oh god, Al'frind?" Her face switches from annoyance to pain.

"He's gone, Opal," I say bitterly.

"He tried to save me, you know. He's dead *because of me*." Opal lets a fat tear roll down her alabaster cheek.

"No," I say, kissing her forehead, "he died protecting his queen from a situation she had no control over."

"I'm sorry Ke'ain."

Before I can even tell her again it's not her fault, a food vendor approaches us.

"Something warm for the queen," he says, bowing his head.

The silver bowl is full of absolutely mouth watering sq'aurks.

"The queen doesn't like—"

"Thank you," she says as she accepts the bowl I know disgusts her.

As the fi'len man walks away to pass out more of the delicacy to the crash survivors, I turn to my wife. "You don't have to eat that, you know."

"There's a lot of things I know I don't have to do, but bubble babe Opal is a different beast than Queen of Sontafrul 6 Opal. When my subjects give me a gift, I might as well be gracious enough to try it." She takes a steadying breath.

I laugh as she brings the two pronged pick with a pale pink sq'aurk up to her mouth. She pops it in quickly and braces herself for the worst.

As she chews, though, her face slowly softens. "Ke'ain!"

"Are you all right?" I check her over once more in a panic. *Are humans allergic to sq'aurks?*

"Sq'aurks taste exactly like peach pie!" she squeals with delight.

"Looks like I can let Gra'eth off the hook about sourcing an Earth pie for you, can't I?" I breathe a sigh of relief.

She shovels the pastel puff balls in her mouth. I smile as her red human blood floods back into her face.

"I don't think I'll ever be able to leave you alone again," I say.

"Ke'ain, I'm fine." She sets a blue sq'aurk in front of my lips.

I pop the delicious morsel into my mouth. "So these taste like Earth peaches?"

"Even better, peach pie. I want them every day."

"I can arrange that."

Opal hands me the empty bowl and rises to her feet, somewhat shakily. She moves into the crowd and I follow close behind.

Wrapped in nothing more than a blanket, the fi'len still know their queen.

"Thank you," she whispers to each fi'len nursing a soaked and half-drowned human woman.

They bow their heads, accepting their queen's praise reverently.

When she arrives at Gra'eth and his red-maned human, I have to remind myself that he saved Opal as she embraces him with her whole body.

"Thank you Gra'eth. I know you don't like me, but thank you all the same."

He stiffens when he sees me try my best to shove my hands into my pockets.

"Opal, just because you're the weird alien who stole my best friend's heart doesn't mean I dislike you." Gra'eth smartly pushes the queen away and against me. "But just for future reference, if you touch me like that again, your mate is going to have to kill me. We *really* do need to get you some classes on fi'len customs, my dear queen." He laughs nervously.

Opal turns to the other human. "And you, thank god your big old brain's been paying attention to this alien tech." She gives the other woman the same crushing hug.

"Sure anytime, um, Your Highness?" she asks, looking toward me.

"Girl, let's just stick with Opal for now." She giggles, the sound of which eases the adrenaline still pumping through my veins. Opal is safe.

"Sounds good, as long as we don't have to reenact the movie *Speed* ever again, I'll do whatever you say."

"Jessy, this is Ke'ain." Opal pulls me to her, and I look at the woman's extended hand.

"Opal, do you wish for me to touch another woman?" I ask, concerned. Maybe the crash course in fi'len mate customs is something I should prioritize for my new bride.

Opal rolls her eyes. "Jesus fuck, you can't even shake her hand? There are some customs that humans do, you're just going to have to get over," she says in a patronizing tone as she places the other woman's palm into mine.

"Thank you Jessy," I say, even though my mate bond makes me want to rip my hand from hers.

"No problem, Keanu. You've got yourself a real Sandra Bullock there! You know, like the movie *Speed*? Get it?"

Jessy is absolutely cracking up as she turns to Gra'eth as if he's ever even seen a human movie.

"Opal, what is—"

"Don't worry about it, big guy. Let's get all these gals to the palace." She gestures to all the humans with their fi'len saviors. "Then I want to blow the Deenz out of the fucking universe."

She turns to Gra'eth, gingerly touching the bracelet on her wrist. "Tell the war council to close the borders. No one gets in or out until I find the assholes who killed Al'frind."

"You got it boss," he says nervously, looking my way.

Opal reaches her hand to Jessy. "Come on, I've got a bed with your name on it back at the castle."

Jessy stops and lets Opal pull her arm taut.

"I thought maybe I'd stay with Gray Seth here...I mean, if that's okay with him. I don't want to be a bother when you've got all this other stuff going on," she mumbles as she looks back toward Gra'eth.

His blue eyes light up, and I smirk as I realize what's going through his head.

"Gra'eth?" Opal frowns. "Surely he's got too much on his plate—"

I pull my bride away from them before she can protest much more.

"Let a fi'len stay with his mate, won't you?" I whisper through clenched teeth as soon as we're out of earshot.

"Wait? Jessy is Gra'eth's mate?" She knits her brows as she turns her head to glance at the pair. "You really think so?"

I look back over my shoulder too and see my calloused friend break out in a blue blush. "Oh yeah. Jessy might not know it yet, but I think Gra'eth might have an inkling."

Opal laughs with her whole chest. "That poor man." She bites her lips between her teeth and feigns a wince. It's quickly replaced by a menacing smile. "So, ready to get those hive-minded bastards and make them pay?"

"Whatever it takes to make sure you and our newest subjects are safe, I'll do."

As I help Opal into the tactical cruiser, a gray hand taps my shoulder. I spin to find one of the medics.

"My king," he says as he pulls down his face mask and bows.

"Can I help you Medic..." I check his name badge. "Hi'rey?"

"I thought I should let you know, the queen is with child." He grabs my hand in a congratulatory shake. "The goddess has truly blessed your union."

I turn my head to see my bride, but Opal is too far into the cruiser to hear the news.

"We thought that might not be biologically possible. Are you quite sure?" I ask.

"I'm not a human expert, but our data pad scan confirmed it," he says confidently.

"Can you do me a favor, Hi'rey? Keep this information to yourself until the palace has time to process the best way to share this information, won't you?" I ask.

"Of course, Your Majesty." He nods. "Congratulations. May the goddess bless you with a healthy heir."

"Thank you," I told him, still in shock.

Opal? *Pregnant.* Me? *A father.*

The Deenz are done for. I place my hand on Opal's stomach as I take my seat next to her.

"You are the most perfect thing I've ever seen, you know that?"

"I better be." She arches an eyebrow as she settles into the seat and closes her eyes.

CHAPTER 15
☆NO STRINGS ATTACHED☆

☆GRA'ETH

JESSY, the spotted human with a red mane, is a peculiar creature. As we sit in my cruiser, she pokes at the upholstered panels and wedges her finger into any spot it'll fit.

"What are you doing?" I ask.

She pulls her hands back into her lap and clasps them together quickly, like a scolded child. "Oh sorry, sometimes I just get the urge to see how things work." She sighs. "You know, to see the man behind the curtain and all the jazz."

I frown. "What curtain?"

"Ah yes, I must make a mental note to be quite literal with you, Gray Seth. Human pop culture obviously isn't your strong suit," she rambles softly under her breath.

I run my eyes up her torso. She's shaped much differently than the only other human I've known—my queen, Opal.

Opal is all soft roundness while Jessy is much leaner. I hate to say it, but also a bit unwieldy with her long limbs. She's *interesting* visually, I won't deny that.

Her personality is the strange part. I feel like she is appraising me with every glance.

165

"Do you have a swim bladder, Seth?" She cocks her head as she runs her eyes down my bare chest—my shirt and jacket lost in the shuffle.

"Excuse me?" I raise my eyebrows. What kind of question is that? "Do you?"

"No need to get testy there, Gray Seth." She raises a palm to pacify me. "I don't have a swim bladder, seeing as humans are terrestrial animals. Not trying to be rude, just curious is all."

She pushes her fingers into her mouth and bites the cuticle of her index finger. I can smell the blood blooming from her self-inflicted wound.

"Stop it," I say, pulling her hands roughly from her mouth.

"Wow, okay Dad," she says as she rolls her eyes.

"It's just…" I search for the correct words, but am not sure I find them. "You shouldn't hurt yourself like that."

"It's not a big deal," she says, clenching her mouth tightly.

"I can smell the blood."

"Really?" Her eyes light up as she looks at the speck of blood welling at the corner of her cuticle. "Such a small amount?"

"You can't smell that?" I wrinkle my nose at the blast of iron coming from her finger.

"Not at all. I bet I smell awful though—I haven't had a decent shower in a long time. Just the decon spray as needed, ya know?"

I bite the inside of my cheek to stop the anger rising in my chest. The Deenz treated these human women like livestock.

"Do you want a shower? I could help you with that."

Jessy arches an eyebrow. "You know, I really was just a dancer…I rarely got picked for the extra stuff."

It's a good thing her human senses are so dull, otherwise she might smell the tang of my own blood filling my mouth. I unclench my jaw, trying my hardest not to think of what those purple ingrates did to her.

"I wasn't propositioning you, just so we're on the same page," I say. "I have a shower unit at my apartment in the palace. You're welcome to use it, by yourself, no strings attached."

"Mighty nice of you there, Seth." She runs a finger under her armpit and sniffs it, wrinkling her nose. "Is that where we're heading now? Because I think I'll take you up on it."

I shift uncomfortably in my seat, trying to find the best way to adjust my cock without drawing attention to myself. The same scent that has Jessy making disgusted faces hits me in a completely different way.

Is there some weird human fever fi'len are susceptible to? I don't want to think of all the off world germs Jessy is likely carrying. It doesn't seem like the right moment to bring up possible decontamination procedure. I'd already be f'teed at this point after sharing air with her.

Her lips felt so soft. I shake my head, trying to focus.

"My name is Gra'eth–not Gray Seth, not Seth." I form the syllables slowly with my mouth. "GRAHHH'EHHHTH."

I hope she's distracted by my lips as I cross my legs away from her.

"Oh, well, I like Seth better." She turns back to her inspection of the cruiser. "Do you know what they're going to do with us?".

"What do you mean 'do with you'?" I ask.

"Like where my place might be here. If I get any say, I think I'd like to retire from the entertainment industry, if at all possible." Jessy's hand slides back up to her lips and she chews on her fingernails again. "But if that's not an option, I'll do what I have to as long as I stay safe, I suppose."

Jessy, the strange little half-naked human sitting in my cruiser, is ready to do what she needs to so no one hurts her.

"No one is going to hurt you here," I say cooly.

I catch a flash of her wet eye before she stealthily wipes it.

"I learned a long time ago there's no way to guarantee my safety anymore."

Before I can stop my body's reaction, my hand drifts to the back of her neck and traces the bone at the base.

167

"I can guarantee your safety," I say in a tone I hope reads of sincerity to her human mind.

She...She *flinches* at my touch.

I quickly withdraw my hand. "I'm sorry."

"It's okay, big guy, just haven't had any good touches recently, ya know?" she whispers. "No strings attached to that offer, just for clarification?"

If by no strings attached, she means I'll keep making a goddess damned fool of myself. That I'll have to focus to keep from grabbing her head and huffing the scent of her glorious mane. That'd I'd rip the throat of any man who looks at her too long.

"*Sure,* no strings attached."

☆EPILOGUE: THREE MONTHS LATER☆

☆OPAL

I SLIDE my arms out of my ceremonial robe and cradle my heavy belly as I enter my bathing chambers.

"Anything else we can assist you with, my queen?" Jes'inth asks.

"I'm fine, thank you, Jes'inth," I say as I step into the large tr'ael tub full of warm soapy water. It sluices up my thighs and warms my tired joints deliciously.

We've made some fantastic progress at eradicating the Deenz. We've outed them to the Universal Governing Senate and stopped the trafficking of humans from Earth.

Every day, we're picking up new clusters of human women—saving them from a life of slavery. I've even turned one of the palace's many wings into what the refugees call "Earth 2."

It's a bit like walking into a sorority house, and that hasn't been without its issues. It turns out that when you pick up a bunch of random Earthwomen, they're not guaranteed to get along.

Some of us have made Sontafrul 6 our new home. A few of the women from the crash were mated to their rescuers. I still can't say I understand the fi'len mate bond—but shit, those alien men sure do. They seem to know the second it kicks into motion.

Some women are a little dubious, but some of them were so starved for love and safety that they jumped right into the mate relationship.

It's kind of wild that the fi'len seem to be so compatible with us. I look down at my swollen belly. At three months along, I look closer to eight months in human gestation terms. *Maybe a little too compatible.*

I might not have picked this exact moment in time to become a mom, but damn, I sure do want to have the big gray guy's kids. Since we've found out that fi'len sperm seems to have no issue navigating the human reproductive system, we've had to teach the women how to use the weird alien prophylactics. I thought Medic Hi'rey was going to die of embarrassment when the auditorium full of human woman giggled as he brought out a to-scale model of a fi'len penis and showed how to apply the seed sheath. Serves him right for telling Ke'ain about my pregnancy before me. The fi'len obviously have nothing similar to HIPAA.

I've been under constant medical supervision, as we're not exactly sure when I'll pop. The fi'len gestation is much shorter, about three months, compared to our nine. At my checkup this morning, the medics confirmed the baby would be viable outside my body.

As I lean back into the tub, my aching back is forever grateful we're almost done. The water makes me feel weightless, and I savor that feeling and close my eyes.

The door cracks open, and I know exactly who it is. My big gray husband drops his trousers to the ground.

"I heard something interesting today from your friend Jessy," he says as he scoots me forward and slides into the tub behind me.

"It better be good if you're disturbing my incredibly relaxing bath." I yawn. "You know, I think this baby is taking after you. It feels huge!"

Ke'ain laughs. "I think you'll enjoy this bit of information."

He slides a hand around to play with my pussy.

"Oh?" I arch my hips into his palm.

"I mentioned that our baby is fully formed, and she told me about a human tradition."

"What human tradition is that?" I palm my breast, which, thanks to this pregnancy, is more sensitive than ever.

"That when humans are due, they eat spicy food and mate to speed up the baby's arrival." He kisses my neck and pushes two of his large fingers into me.

"So, no spicy food for me?" I gasp as he probes into me.

"I figured we'd try mating a few times first." He pulls me higher onto his chest.

He removes his fingers from inside me and softly strokes my clit, his free hand moving to his already hard cock. He roughly milks it as he places it right at my entrance.

"Fuck, Ke'ain," I moan as he pushes his throbbing length deeper.

"That's what I'm trying to do, Opal," he says as he grabs my ass.

Even without the water, I would have no doubt he could lift me quickly, but this alien has a way of making my huge pregnant ass feel petite even without the extra buoyancy.

As he spears into me again, I moan as his sucker finds its new favorite place. It grips and pops over my ass.

Although the sucker hasn't been able to reach my clit recently, I can't say I hate this new development. I would generally say I'm not an ass girl, but I don't know if it's the extra blood flow or that I've become a pregnancy nympho, but it feels like an itch I've never had the pleasure of scratching.

As Ke'ain thrusts into me, I recline fully on his chest.

Moving his hands to my breasts, he breathes into my ear. "I'll miss these. I think their growth might be my favorite part of human reproduction."

I drive myself down onto his shaft, and when he's fully seated, he hits a part of me that no human man ever could. I grind my ass into the sweet sucker and move my hand to my clit.

"Do you want to feel me come around your cock, babe?" I arch as much as possible, and Ke'ain supports my stomach as I move.

"Yes," he breathes.

His voice sends bursts of serotonin to my brain. I pull myself forward, with all the grace of a newborn giraffe, until I'm on my knees.

"Well then fuck me, like you mean it," I say over my shoulder.

Ke'ain shifts to his knees, the soapy water sloshing onto the floor as he displaces it with his hulking form. A light in his eyes tells me I'm about to be fucked into next week, and I wiggle my ass to egg him on.

Ke'ain grabs his cock and wastes no time finding home as he plows into me. Gone are the "Did I hurt you?" or "Is the baby okay?" from earlier in my pregnancy.

Even if this is just some ploy to induce labor, I will do my damndest to enjoy it.

When he slides into me, my breath catches in my throat. He pulls back and slams into me once more.

"Is this what you want...my queen?" he growls.

Ke'ain places a hand between my legs and finds my clit in a pinching motion. With each crash of his body, his sucker stimulates between the cheeks, and he pushes his fucking perfect cock as far as it'll go. I'm undone with a final flick of his fingers.

I brace myself against the side of the tub and let the pleasure surge through me. I swear I can feel my bones melt as he pulls me back into him.

"Think we're any closer to meeting them?" Ke'ain asks as I try to catch my breath.

"Maybe we should try again?" I tilt my chin up and look at the fucking alien sex god I somehow get to spend the rest of my life with.

"As many times as we need to, I suppose." He sighs as he moves my rag doll body to our bedroom. He gently sets me on the bed and pushes my knees apart.

"I wanted dessert anyway," is the last thing I hear from him before his head disappears behind my bump.

☆AUTHOR'S NOTE☆

In the ever eloquent words of Opal, "Jesus Fuck!" is probably the best expletive for how I feel completing this book. AIWWSBIGABAI came out of nowhere. Right after I finished *The Dropped Stitch: Transformation*, I decided to give a friend's writing prompts on discord a whirl to cleanse my author palette. The first prompt I wrote is chapter one of this book. In fact, you might find it funny to know that nearly every chapter in this book is a writing prompt. The characters were just begging to be written, so I did my best.

This is so different from anything I ever thought I would write, but as someone who is a bit of a class clown, the ability to use humor as much as I did made it all the more enjoyable. Speaking of humor, my husband has two nicknames for Ke'ain. The first one that made it into the book is Keanu, the second one which didn't make it in is Shart-boy. Mind you both are said with love, and I want to thank him for putting up with my ramblings on alien erotica during the creation of this book.

I also wanted to thank the several members of the discord where those writing prompts were posted who truly hyped up my writing, fought over who was Ke'ain's IRL girlfriend, and placed themselves in Opal's shoes for all the best smutty scenes.

Specifically Momma, Nicole, Emilia, and Krysten.

And thank you to *you*, dear reader, for hopefully enjoying this wild ride.

It goes without saying that my ever patient editors deserve thanks. Both Jessica Netzke and Emily Michel help to turn my grammatical nightmare into a novella.

To all my arc readers, you are the best.

I didn't want to leave the world I built with Ke'ain and Opal, **so I decided not to**. After I complete writing *The Dropped Stitch 3*, hopefully this month, I've already got book two of the Bubble Babes series lined up and ready to go. You probably guessed from the last chapter who that couple might be!

I'm excited to pair up Gra'eth's sarcasm with Jessy's dorkiness.

It'll be a different match up from our King and Queen of Sontafrul 6, that's for sure! I don't know if I'm done with Opal and Ke'ain's story either, but it feels complete for now. They'll pop up in other books in the series, as will some of their rulings and dealings with the Deenz.

But I'm glad they got their happy-for-now ending.

XOXO, PETRA

☆ GLOSSARY ☆

Fi'len Words

- **F'tee:** An expletive, similar to our English fuck
- **Thr'uik:** Fi'leen liquor
- **Sq'aurks:** Pastel puff balls that are eaten alive. They steam and are hot naturally. They taste like peach pie according to Opal. Delicacy.
- **Si'bok:** A large ceremonial water vehicle. Kind of like a yacht. Used only for parades.
- **Grin'oj:** A fi'len child's breakfast food. Served with cinnamon. Opal thinks it tastes like sweetened mashed potatoes.
- **Waters of I'loh:** The glowing and warm waters that flow through underground springs through all of Sontafrul 6. Are said to have healing/magical properties. I'loh is a major goddess of the fi'len faith.
- **Tr'ael:** Black shiny mineral of Sontafrul 6. The old palace is made entirely of a natural outcropping, the rooms being carved in. Also the rock that the bracelet Al'frind gave Opal. Opal often refers to it as ebony.
- **Ckra'rot:** Large feathered bird.

- **Cor'sopol:** Color shifting alien
- **Poke'en:** Tentacled stinging creature that lives in the seas of Sontafrul 6
- **Mals'in Tree:** Tree that's foliage shifts from bright pink to pale orange throughout the year. Similar to a palm tree.

Misc.

- **Security Bubble:** Large acrylic oval-shaped bubbles that human woman are placed in for their protection.
- **The Deenz:** Hive-minded aliens, traffickers of human women, cheap slimy assholes.
- **Go-Go Juice/Hormone Shot:** aphrodisiac shot given to human women by the Deenz before performances.
- **Cruiser:** Magnetic vehicle that can only drive on mag lanes.
- **Transport Unit:** Bus-like cruiser that can only drive on mag lanes.
- **Tactical Cruiser:** Jet-propelled vehicle used most by dignitaries and the military. Is not bound by the mag lanes.
- **Protein Ration:** Seafood-based protein bar given to the military as rations.
- **Data pad:** Alien tech that is almost like an iPad, and can make calls like a communicator.
- **Communicator:** Alien cell phone.
- **Decon Tech:** Someone who specializes in decontaminating aliens from potential world-killer viruses.
- **Universal Governing Senate:** The governing system for advanced life forms in the universe. Humans are not considered advanced.

☆OUR CAST OF CHARACTERS☆

These descriptions are at of the END of this book. If you read this before you finish reading the book you might spoil it for yourself–be warned!

- **Opal:** Kentucky girl abducted from Earth. Both parents are dead, former waitress at the Crafty Crab. At the end of this book is the Queen Of Sontafrul 6 and is married/mated to Ke'ain.
- **Ke'ain:** King of Sontafrul 6, married/mated to Opal. Really likes sq'aurks, but not as much as Opal's cunt. AKA Sharkboy, AKA Keanu.
- **Jessy:** Former NASA rocket scientist from Cape Canaveral. Neurodivergent and analytical. Has been gone from Earth for years. Is respected among the bubble babes and kind of like the house Mom.
- **Gra'eth:** Royal attorney for Sontafrul 6's monarchy. At the end of this book is also hand of the king. Saves Opal and Jessy from drowning in the bus crash. Ke'ain's right hand man. Sarcastic and sick of everyone's shit. Germaphobe. AKA Gray Seth.
- **The King and Queen of Sontafrul 6:** Ke'ains parents who died in the events of this book. The king is a

greedy man and has let Sontafrul 6 go to shit with pollution from tourists. Neither of them are particularly great parents to Ke'ain.

- **Al'frind:** Ke'ain's personal royal butler, but more of a father figure to him. Old and wise fi'len man. He dedicated his life to Ke'ain when the prince was born– the day after his mate Jas'ryn's death. Is killed by the Deenz in the events of this book.

- **Raf'ere:** Ke'ain's cousin and ruler of the Liin'gan Reefs on Sontafrul 6. Is arrogant and pigheaded with a huge ego. He rescues Opal and Ke'ain from the island the maurader's stranded them on. He is one of Ke'ains few living relatives after the death of his parents.

- **Tro'kip:** Ke'ain's wetnurse and nanny. Died before the start of this book. His true mother figure.

- **Officer Hy'rul:** A member of Raf'ere's cruiser staff.

- **Jes'inth:** One of Opal's lady's maids once she becomes Queen of Sontafrul 6.

- **Medic Hi'rey:** The first person to know that Opal is pregnant. Has to teach the women living in the "Earth 2" sorority house how to use alien condoms.

- **Captain Fer'oon:** Fi'len marauder, mysterious background. Seems to have biomech modifications-his face is half covered by a mask. Has black hair, unlike the other fi'len's white hair.

- **Saniri:** A marauder who hates slavery. Snake-like alien who seems best suited to a desert.

- **Unnamed Marauder:** A little bit slow on the uptake, this green goon is very bad at following instructions of his captain.

☆THE BUBBLE-VERSE

My ebooks are exclusive to Amazon, but my physical copies are available at Amazon and your favorite book retailers. If it's not available at your bookstore, request it!

All I Wanted Was Sushi But I Got Abducted By Aliens Instead: Bubble Babes #1

2023

All I Wanted Was To Become A Scientist But Now I've Got An Alien Boyfriend: Bubble Babes #2

2023

☆COMING SOON

Bubble Babes #3

ESTIMATED PUBLICATION 2023

Bubble Babes #4

ESTIMATED PUBLICATION 2024

Soldiers Of Sontafrul 6 #1

ESTIMATED PUBLICATION 2024

☆WANT MORE NOW?

PATREON [https://www.patreon.com/petrapalerno]

I've got some short stories and other bonus content (including very NSFW art of our lovely couples) on my Patreon! There's also a tier on where you can vote on a monthly bonus chapter for your favorite couple!

ETSY [https://www.etsy.com/shop/petrapalerno]

Art, stickers, page overlays, and other fun goodies are available here!

Printed in the USA
CPSIA information can be obtained
at www.ICGtesting.com
LVHW050606041123
762866LV00079B/2811